D09955391

THE SUMMER OF JUNE

ALSO BY JAMIE SUMNER

One Kid's Trash
Roll with It
Tune It Out

THE SUMMER OF JUNE

JAMIE SUMNER

ATHENEUM BOOKS FOR YOUNG READERS
New York London Toronto Sydney New Delhi

ATHENEUM BOOKS FOR YOUNG READERS
An imprint of Simon & Schuster Children's Publishing Division
1230 Avenue of the Americas, New York, New York 10020

For information about special discounts for bulk purchases, please contact Simon & Schuster
Special Sales at 1-866-506-1949 or business@simonandschuster.com.
The Simon & Schuster Speakers Bureau can bring authors to your live event. For more information
or to book an event, contact the Simon & Schuster Speakers Bureau at 1-866-248-3049 or visit our
website at www.simonspeakers.com.
Interior design by Karyn Lee
The text for this book was set in Georgia.
Manufactured in the United States of America
0422 FFG
First Edition
10 9 8 7 6 5 4 3 2 1
Library of Congress Cataloging-in-Publication Data
Names: Sumner, Jamie, author.
Title: The summer of June / Jamie Sumner.
Description: First edition. | New York : Atheneum Books for Young Readers, [2022] | Audience:
Ages 10 and Up. | Summary: Eleven-year-old June is determined to beat her anxiety and become
the lion she knows she is, instead of the mouse everyone sees, and with the help of Homer Juarez,
the poetry-reciting soccer star, she starts a secret library garden and hatches a plan to make her
dreams come true.
Identifiers: LCCN 2021036500 | ISBN 9781534486027 (hardcover) | ISBN 9781534486041
(ebook)
Subjects: CYAC: Anxiety disorders—Fiction. | Mothers and daughters—Fiction. | Friendship—
Fiction. | Gardening—Fiction.
Classification: LCC PZ7.1.S8545 Su 2022 | DDC [Fic]—dc23
LC record available at https://lccn.loc.gov/2021036500

For my mom—
my first and best librarian

"But there is a third thing you must do . . .
you must do something to make the world more beautiful."
—BARBARA COONEY, *Miss Rumphius*

THE
SUMMER
OF JUNE

Behold

I AM A WONDER TO BEHOLD.

At least, that's what Mom said when she saw the clumps of hair on the bathroom floor. She took one look at my bald head and my bare feet itching under all that shed weight and announced, "Junebug, you are a wonder to behold." And then she pried the pink Bic razor from my fingers and took it to her own head. That's the thing about Mom. She is a woman of action.

Her dark waves fell and mixed with my blond ones, and altogether we made an unruly mess. But it was a mess on the floor and not on our heads, so that was that.

She was not a wonder to behold. Honestly.

All that hair had been hiding bumps and divots and a scalp so white it was almost gray. She scratched at it with her glittery purple nails, exploring the whole craggy moonscape.

"Mom, you look sensational," I said, our brown eyes

hooking on each other in the mirror. It was not true. Sometimes you have to tell a little lie to call a bigger truth into being. This summer I am summoning *all* our truths.

Truth #1: I will not be the girl who pulls out her own hair because she's running from the anxious thoughts in her head.

Truth #2: Mom and I will own our power as fierce, independent females.

Just because her boyfriend, Keith, dumped her last week does not mean Mom has to turn into the lonesome librarian. He wasn't even supposed to be her boyfriend in the first place. He stopped by to try to sell us insurance and stayed three years! We can be happy without him. Together. On our own.

Here's Truth #3 (the secret truth): I am tired of being the nervous mouse girl who is scared all the time and runs from everything. And I'm sick of waiting for the right things to happen. This summer, I am going to be a *lion*. And I will make happily ever after come to me.

Ten minutes later:

I stand in front of my dresser mirror and stare at my "melon," as Mom calls it. I hate my hair. Mom lied. I am no wonder. I look like a visitor from another planet. I feel like that all the time, but now my outsides match my insides and I'm not okay with it. I turn my head left and then right, but the view's no better. I'm no lion. I am a pale white thing in a pale white room. I turn away from the mirror before I have to watch myself cry.

My head itches to be itched, but I tuck my fingers into my palms. That's what got me in trouble in the first place. First the itch starts on the inside, from all the prickly thoughts, and then it spreads outside like a creeping vine until I can feel it all over me, like poison ivy. So I scratch. But once I start, I can't stop. And then the scratching isn't enough. So I pull. I yank and yank until, with a tiny satisfying ping of pain, a hair or five come away. For a sweet second, I'm numb. The worries go quiet. I can stop rocking in place. I can be still, inside and out.

What nobody gets is that hair-pulling is satisfying with a capital *S*. Each strand is a pull-chain in the tub. Yank on it and a little of the worry leaks out. It keeps me from overflowing . . . or it did. I knock on my bare head with my fist, once, gently, like I'm knocking on a door. *Hello, anybody home?* This was a colossal mistake. Why did I think that because my hair is gone the itchy worry would be too? What am I going to do when it starts and I've got nothing to use to stop it? Can you drown in your own thoughts?

I pace, following the swirls in the grain of the wood floor, back and forth, back and forth. There is a patch of morning light in the shape of a diamond. I stop. Crouch. Stick my hand over it so the diamond is on my palm. It is warm as a hug. I wish I could carry it with me, that warm patch of light.

"Junebug, you better be dressed and on the curb in two minutes!" Mom yells from the kitchen just as the toaster oven dings. I can smell the cinnamon and butter from here. Mom makes an excellent croissant French toast, which most of the time we eat in plastic bags filled with syrup in the car. We are always late. It's the most dependable thing about us.

When I settle onto the cracked leather of Thelma's interior, the tag from my T-shirt slides up, touching a spot on my neck I did not know existed. I flinch. I did not anticipate the tag issue. Without my hair in the way, it is a lightning rod, a buzzer to my senses like that game Operation, where you have to pull out the organs with tiny tweezers. I tug at my collar while Thelma coughs and rumbles and sighs. When Mom curses her whole existence, Thelma finally vrooms to life. Thelma's our Ford. She used to be red, we think, but now she's mostly rust—the color of a rotten orange. But we love her. Seven years ago, she got us all the way from New Orleans to Nashville. Thelma is the means of all our great escapes.

Ants go marching up and down my back. No, it's just the tag. I wriggle my shoulders up and down, up and down. My therapist, Gina, likes to say my mind has a mind of its own. It fixates on the strangest and most unreasonable things. I worry about the tag. I worry that I will keep worrying about the tag. I worry that it worries me. It is the worry-go-round, a hamster on a wheel.

I try my favorite car trick to stop the thoughts. I crack my window and let the wind blow straight in my eyes until they fill with tears and the maple trees blur, their green leaves waving like peacock feathers. I would like to be a peacock—so bright and beautiful that people are drawn to me.

Mom rolls her own window all the way down too. She finds a Ray LaMontagne song on the radio. I don't know how she can seem so easy in herself, with her hand out the window riding the waves of the wind. She is the yin to my yang.

Nick, Mr. Ex #2, was a musician, and he sounded just like Ray on the radio. He is how we ended up in Nashville in the first place. He lasted the longest, ages four to eight in "June time," but he was also the worst. He was the slowest to realize that nobody can stick with Mom without getting me in the bargain. When he finally showed himself for what he was, Mom kicked him to the curb. But it was too late for me. Not all shadows dissolve in the sunshine. He's been my shadow for years. But I don't like to talk about that.

We're only a five-minute drive to the Columbia Public Library, where Mom works. It's just south of the teeny tiny downtown of Franklin that has been our home these past seven years just outside Nashville. At ten till ten on this Saturday morning, we pull into the library's parking lot, more potholes than road, and bump along to the employee slots under the row of crab-apple trees around back. I tip the plastic baggie into my mouth and suck out the last few drops of syrup.

"Ick, June." Mom shudders.

I smack my lips. "Don't yuck my yum."

Like bank robbers, we kick Thelma's doors open and launch ourselves out, bald heads and all, into the damp morning heat. Summer, here we come.

2
Juveniles

THE LIBRARY DOES NOT KNOW IT'S THE FIRST DAY of summer vacation and therefore smells as it always does, like circulated air and dust and lemony wood polish. I love it.

But I do *not* love Mrs. Tandy's angry red mouth and clickety fingernails on the high wooden checkout counter as she watches the automatic doors swish closed behind us. Mrs. Tandy is in charge of the whole library. She darts between the juvenile and teen and DVD sections so she can sneak up on you like the world's worst hall monitor if you so much as tip something out of place. If she catches you, she sucks air between her teeth so it makes a wet whistling sound and barks, "May I help you?" in a way that leaves only one answer: "No." She is a bird of prey. And right now she has got her beady eyes aimed at our bald heads.

The Tandy, as I like to call her, clicks her fingernails.

"Ms. Delancey, may I see you for a moment?"

"Wait right here, baby girl. I'll be back in a hot second," Mom says, and winks at me. Her big brown eyes look even bigger without all that hair. I wonder if mine do too. No way I'm finding a mirror to check. I've had enough of my own reflection today. I run a hand over my scalp as Mom walks away, her skirt swishing and sandals jingling. Mom should be on a beach somewhere with me, not following the Tandy into the cave-dark sorting room.

The library is technically not open yet, so I have the whole lobby to myself. I wander over to the recent returns cart. It's my favorite shelf-that-is-not-a-shelf in the whole library. These are the books that are so newly brought back, they haven't been sorted yet. You can find a Rachael Ray cookbook leaning against a John Grisham paperback that's propping up six Llama Llama books. Sometimes there is an atlas of ancient Greece or a leather-bound encyclopedia, covering letters *X, Y, Z*, and it makes me want to meet the person who skipped Google and chose that instead. What was their impetus? "Impetus: a moving force; impulse; stimulus." I learned *that* from a Webster's thesaurus found on this very shelf last November. There was a lot of time to fill over Thanksgiving break.

Unlike all the other shelves in the library that are already sorted, this one has no order. It's the place you go when you don't know what you want. For me, that's almost always. I once found a Dr. Seuss book about two towns fighting over which side to butter your bread on, top or bottom. I took it home to experiment. I toasted two big slices of Mom's sourdough and tried it both ways. It turns out I am a butter-side-down girl. All thanks to Dr. Seuss and the recent returns.

Today's selection is slim. I sift through *Watership Down, Computer Programming for Dummies, Harry Potter and the Goblet of Fire,* and a how-to knitting book. If they all came from the same person, that would be someone I would want to know.

I shiver under the air-conditioning and pull my T-shirt up higher on my neck. It's so much colder without hair. But then the tag starts to bother me again and I tug it down. But that feels wrong too and I can't stop my fingers from yanking at the neck of my shirt, tugging it all out of shape. As Mom comes swishing out of the sorting cave, I grab the knitting book and tuck it under my arm to give my hands something to do. She has an ugly scarf with big brown-and-orange swirls all over it wrapped around her head. She looks like a grandma ready for bingo. Ick.

"What is that?" she asks, pointing to my knitting book.

"What is *that*?" I ask, pointing to her head.

She sighs and steers me by the elbow up the stairs to

the teen section, where she is the head librarian. It is like day versus night up here compared to downstairs. She has strung fairy lights so she doesn't have to turn on the overhead fluorescents that make your eyeballs ache. And in the center of the room there is a big round rug that's designed to look like you're staring into the bottom of a well. I call it the wishing rug.

She also keeps extra chargers for iPads and iPhones and laptops and whatever else you could need in her desk, and she lets anyone borrow them anytime they want. And she has read every YA fantasy/thriller/rom-com in existence. Basically, she is the coolest librarian there ever was, and she's not even a real librarian. She never went to school for it or anything, but the Tandy's so prickly, people don't tend to hang around for long. When the last librarian quit four years ago, Mom's friend Sharika got her the job, and she's been here ever since.

"The Tandy made you put that on, didn't she?" I say the minute we get to her desk.

Mom sighs. "Don't call her that, and yes, she did. She said I needed to look more professional."

We study her orange-and-brown head in the reflection of her computer monitor. She starts laughing first, and so I don't feel so bad joining in.

"Oh, heaven help me, that is awful," she says, ripping off the scarf and shoving it in the bottom drawer of her desk. She scratches at her neck, which makes me scratch.

"Honey, no."

She sets a cool hand on my neck, capturing my fingers. "I like our new look. We're a team, remember? The Tandy can deal with it."

I sniff. "I thought you said we couldn't call her that."

"Well, some rules are worth breaking."

She leans in and gives me a kiss right on the top of my head. It's strange, being kissed there on my bare skin. It sends shivers down my spine, but it settles my mind a bit. That's Mom's magic—she is a June-soother.

Overhead, we hear the Tandy screech out the announcements for the day. *"Children's story time at ten-thirty and one. Understanding online safety for tweens at four,"* taught by the Tandy and not Mom, which means no one will come. *"Cookbook club at six."*

I nudge Mom. "You should go to that."

She rolls her eyes. "I'm off at six. We'll go have us a cookbook party at home."

I roll my eyes back at her.

Mom is a great cook. It's her second-favorite thing, after me and before books. In fact, she was in cooking school on her way to being a professional pastry chef back in New Orleans. But you can't stay on your feet all day in a hot kitchen in a hotter city when you're nine months pregnant. So there's that. She says she just wasn't cut out for the long hours. But we can all do the math on that one. What's longer: nights in the kitchen of a five-star restaurant or a lifetime caring for another human? All I know is, she makes the flakiest croissants and fluffiest bread pudding the world has ever known. But she won't even go to a free cookbook club.

"Go on, now," she says, shoving me gently toward the door. "Go check on Sharika and report back. Tell her she owes me a dollar if Andy from the Jiffy Lube called."

She's smiling, and kids older than me are starting to trickle in and I know she needs to get to work and she does not want me to worry about her hair or her job or any of the jillions of things I worry about on the regular. So I smile back and it is almost real. I step on the wishing rug on my way out and toss a handful of thoughts down. Here's hoping this is the summer all our wishes come true.

Juveniles, aka the kids' section. Call it whatever you want, but do not pretend there is anything here for an eleven-year-old.

I walk into the big open room with low shelves and tiny chairs and unicorn pillows and am reminded again that I am in the in-between. If you are into puppet shows and scavenger hunts, this is the place to be. But if you're a girl about to step into middle school, too big for story time but too little for zine-making, then you're on your own. If Sharika could have her way, there would be plenty here for me—at least a corner with a comfortable couch or two away from the train table—but we all know the Tandy rules the roost.

I drag my feet past the Shel Silverstein display, where a kid about my age in a faded red T-shirt is sitting cross-legged on the ground like a toddler, his dark hair covering his face. I wander up to the desk.

"Heya, Sharika."

I nod at Sharika, the children's librarian, who is sorting through a box of LEGOs on the counter for a LEGO-building tournament this afternoon. She's in elbows-deep. But when she glances at me, her eyebrows shoot all the way up to her hairline and she jerks back a little.

I am a wonder. I am a wonder. I am a wonder, I repeat to myself.

"Whoa. Bold move."

She is nodding like she likes it, but I think she's in shock. She knows about my hair-pulling, has watched Mom place antibacterial cream on the raw spots, has even sat with me on our bathroom floor when I cried for no reason other than that I had forgotten to put my name on my spelling test and Mrs. Heuerman had taken off five points.

That's the thing about being anxious: it's not always some big thing that triggers it. It can be as small as a quiz grade or rain when you thought it would be sunny or crunchy peanut butter instead of plain or the faucet leaking so you can't stop hearing the *driiiiiip drip, driiiiiip drip*. One time when I was nine, I forgot to say my prayers, which I always said in the same order. When I woke up an hour after bedtime and remembered, I spent the rest of the night hunched under the covers with my hands clasped, whispering the same words over and over: "Dear Lord, please don't let a burglar get in. Please don't let a fire catch on our house. And take care of my mom forever and ever. Thank you. Amen." It was a long night.

Sharika is still staring.

I put a hand to my head and grimace, but she grabs it. I do not love people touching me.

"No. Uh-uh. You've got to hold that beautiful head up high." She touches her own braids, a complicated swirl on the top with pink extensions. "You do you, honey." Easy for her to say. Sharika is the most confident person I know. She doesn't let anyone tell her what's what.

I change the subject.

"Mom wants to know if you owe her a dollar."

Sharika clucks her tongue, leans in, and whispers, "Listen, you tell your mom a call isn't worth a thing if it doesn't come with a date. I need a man with a *plan*."

She starts to laugh, but swallows it when the Tandy comes marching around the corner.

"Is everything ready for story time, Ms. Jones?"

"Oh yes. We've got a good one today. *Ish*, by Peter Reynolds," Sharika replies.

The Tandy leans in closer and Sharika shrinks back. She's the only one who can make Sharika flinch. I get a whiff of rotten flowers. The Tandy's version of perfume, I guess.

"The book about the child who wants to be an artist? Isn't that a little *advanced* for three-year-olds?" she asks, clicking her nails on the counter.

"Well," Sharika says, digging back into her LEGOs and avoiding the Tandy's eye, "I never met a three-year-old who didn't like to draw."

The Tandy huffs and walks away without acknowledging that I was ever here at all.

"That woman," Sharika mutters. But she shakes it off like she always does and points past me to the computers by the Silverstein display. "Why don't you check to see if all our headphones are untangled and plugged in."

Story of my life. No one knows what to do with me, even the good ones like Sharika. Eventually they find a way to say *scram*.

The kid with the dark, curly hair is now lying on the floor in front of the books. He's blocking all the chairs to the computer center. I stand with my hands on my hips for two minutes and thirteen seconds. He does not move or look up. Some people. I kick one of his Nikes. In my flip-flops, it's not as satisfying as I would like. He closes *Where the Sidewalk Ends* as slowly as possible before looking up.

"May I help you?" He pushes a curl out of his eyes and I'm jealous. If I had hair right now, I could hide behind it.

But then I remember I'm supposed to be a lion, so instead I give him my best glare and say, "Yes, you may. Move your giant feet so I can get to these computers."

He lifts himself up on one elbow, but does *not* move his feet. Is he looking at my head? He is. He's looking at my head. Wait, no, I can't tell. My heart pauses and then loses its rhythm.

"'Computers,' plural?" he says from the floor. "Save some for the rest of us."

This kid.

"I am not *using* them. I am *organizing* them," I say, waving my hands around because I don't know what to do with them. It's hard being a lion when you're used to being a mouse.

He sits all the way up, giving me *one inch* of space. It's all I need to squeeze onto the nearest chair and turn my back to him. I feel him stand and move down the row, but I don't look up from the cord I am untangling. Out of the corner of my eye, I see him pick up the headphones at the farthest station and begin to untwist them from the power cord.

"What are you doing?"

"I'm *organizing*." I drop the triple-decker tangle that will not budge. Seriously, they can't tie their shoes, but these kindergarteners can sure make an unbreakable knot. "That is not your job."

He moves one station closer to me. "Is it yours?" he asks, raising one eyebrow without so much as a glance my way.

The best defense is offense. I pretend he does not exist and focus on the task. The more I work, the more my mind stills. I actually forget I'm not alone until we bump arms. I jump like he poked me with a fork.

He hands me the last bunched-up cord. "You do the honors."

I feel him watching and my hands start to shake. There it is, my pulse in my throat like a trapped frog. I can't do it. I can't unravel the cord for all I'm worth. I am about to lose it. I can feel it in the breaths that I can't fully take. I need an exit. Quick. I take a step back and then two and then:

> "'I count myself in nothing else so happy
> As in a soul remembering my good friends.'"

He talks like he's reciting the Pledge of Allegiance and as he does, he slowly but surely unwinds the cord he has taken back from me. It's . . . weird.

"Richard II," he says, and offers me the perfectly straightened cord. I unfreeze my stiff arms and take it. He sticks his hands in his cargo pockets. He is at least half a foot taller than me.

"It's Shakespeare," he adds.

He quotes Shakespeare. Awesome.

"Why'd you say it at me?"

"I didn't say it *at you*."

The silence is thick and sticky as August heat, but he doesn't seem to feel it. I back up to get some space between us because I can't breathe and I'm itching to scratch my head, tug my sleeves, *run*.

He catches me glancing back at the doors and says, all casual and slow, "That was me trying to introduce myself." He smiles and for half a second seems almost shy. "Should've just said hi, I guess. I'm Homer Juarez."

He holds out a hand. I leave it hanging.

"June Delancey."

"Nice to meet you, June," he says.

"Nice knowing you, Homer."

I walk away. The cords are untangled. My job's done. New people are not part of the summer plan. Why does he want to meet *me* anyway? I can feel him staring at my bald head as I leave. I say my truths like a mantra and head for the exit: "Tame the anxiety. Own my independence. Tame the anxiety. Own my independence."

Outside, the sun is so hot it makes the air wavy, and it's not even noon. I lean against the brick wall in the shade. This is going to be one long summer.

3

Seedlings

"YOU ARE CORINNE'S DAUGHTER, YES?"

I open my eyes and squint. A small older man is aiming a knife at me. I close my eyes and try again. He's still there.

"June, right?" he asks, and waves his knife. A clod of dirt falls from it onto my bare toes. It tickles. Funny how a knife doesn't even make my heart skip a beat, while a knotted computer cord undoes me. I guess that's why Gina says worry's not rational.

"Yes, I'm June," I say, and nod.

The old man sticks his knife in the dirt by our feet and holds out a hand. "I am Luis. I have known your mother for several years. She is lovely." He smiles, and his face is an ocean of wrinkles.

Was *lovely*, I think. *Wait until you see the new hairdo.* Luis is still smiling. His eyes are the warmest kind of caramel. He bends over and withdraws the knife, which I see now is not a knife but some sort of gardening implement.

"Would you like to see my zinnias? I have planted them by the bus bench. That is a long wait with nothing to look at but the hedge, don't you think?"

Clearly, Luis is in the mood to talk, as all old people are, except the Tandy, who is probably not human anyway. I don't know what a zinnia is. A flower? A tree? A garden gnome?

Luis smiles and blinks and waits.

I inch toward the entrance to the library. There's sweat dripping down my back, and it's starting to be all I can think about.

"Thanks, Luis. But I think my mom needs me to help set up the beach reads display." This is a lie. Mom hates the term "beach read" and would never create such a display. She thinks any book that is enjoyable should be classified as a couch/beach/tree/car/desk read and leave it at that. But I guess that's too long to put on a sign.

Luis begins to nod and wipe the dirt from his garden knife—spade, that's the word!—on his khaki pants. "Such a good girl, June. Your mother must be very proud."

I wouldn't go that far, I think, and rub my head. I wave goodbye to Luis the spade-carrying bus-stop gardener. But before I can sneak back inside, he places a packet of wildflower seeds into my hand. "For luck," he says. What makes him think I need luck? I don't need luck. I need willpower and to be left alone. I palm the package anyway because I don't want to be rude. But truthfully, I have never grown a thing in my life.

That night, over bowls of carbonara, which is the fancy word Mom uses when I am in charge of dinner and make noodles with butter and cheese, I tell Mom about Luis. Her eyes sparkle like they do when she is thinking up a really good recipe.

"Ah, sweet Luis," she says, twirling her pasta on her spoon. "His wife died last year. I think he's lonely."

"Good thing we've got each other, huh?" I say, because I don't want her missing Keith.

"It is. But you need friends too," she says, pointing her fork at me.

Unfortunately, she knows that me and bathroom stall number three at school have become very close. I can count every brick in the wall and every crack in the windowsill. It's where I hide when school gets to be too much and I need to catch my breath. It's also why I don't have a lot of friends.

I nod into my water glass.

"We have Gina next Tuesday," Mom adds.

"I know. Every week. Spring, summer, fall, winter. Rain or shine. Gina will be waiting."

"Thank God for that," Mom says, ignoring the sarcasm and passing me the dirt pudding. Mom can make chocolate soufflés fluffier than clouds and amaretto cheesecakes that melt in your mouth and fruit tarts shiny with glaze, but my all-time favorite dessert of hers is her ugliest: dirt pudding. But beauty is in the eye of the eater. Give me crushed-up Oreos layered between mounds of vanilla pudding with wriggly gummy worms on top and I am a happy girl.

Later that night when I cannot sleep, *again*, I sneak outside in my bare feet and sit on the back steps. The moon is so big, it feels like you could reach out and touch it. I close my eyes and try not to think about my next visit with Gina. She's going to ask about my hair and how I am "adjusting to a new routine" and whether I have been using those breathing techniques she taught me. I don't want to hurt her feelings, but breathing in for a count of ten is not going to magic me into being a normal kid.

In the white glow of the moon, I study the envelope of seeds that Luis gave me. It's the size of a deck of cards. I tear it open and pour the tiny things into my palm. They look like poppy seeds that have fallen off a bagel. Smaller than a crumb. It seems impossible that something as complicated as a flower could grow from one of these. I pop one into my mouth and chew, trying to feel the floweriness of it on my tongue, but it's so small it's like eating air.

A breeze blows around the corner of the house and I shiver despite the heat. I always get sad this time of night. Mornings are good. But nights have a never-ending feel to them that sits heavy on my chest. It's like the sun might never come up again. Like gravity changes and the world and everything in it sag around the edges. I stand up and open the screen door slowly so it doesn't creak. Before I step inside, I throw the seeds into the trash can and shove the lid down hard. I can't take care of another living thing. I can barely take care of myself.

When I crawl back into bed, I think of Homer with his curly hair and giant feet and Shakespeare. I catch myself hoping I'll see him at the library tomorrow, but then I squash that thought down like I try to do with my worries. I have enough to untangle this summer without another body in the way.

4
Shrinks

I SUPPOSE WE CAN'T HATE KEITH ENTIRELY, I THINK as Thelma thumps along the highway. He did find us Gina. He got her name through his insurance company.

I like Gina. I do—as a person. If she did not have to be my therapist, I'd like her a lot more. She works near the children's hospital in downtown Nashville in an old house someone turned into an office building. Her office is on the top floor, up three creaky flights of stairs. She sits in a white chair in an attic filled with light as if God himself touched his finger to it. Or it could be the skylights.

Keith thought Gina would "cure" me. But after three years of hair-pulling and no sleep and calls home from school when I refused to come out of lucky bathroom stall number three, Keith saw the truth. I am "incurable." At least that's the word he shouted at Mom from the car window before he disappeared in a glow of taillights. Mom doesn't know I heard. But I called Gina and told her. I could hear her clicking her pen on the other end of the line, a sure sign she was worked up but trying to "remain objective." Then she said, "June, you are not 'incurable.' You have the hand you've been dealt, and I am in the business of helping you manage it. Trust me, there's not a single person in the world who doesn't have their own set of problems. *Including* Keith." And then she clicked her pen three more times.

When we get to the office, Mom settles herself in the waiting room with a copy of *Food & Wine* as I make my way up the steps. My sneakers squeak, which bothers me, and the grandfather clock in the lobby is especially loud today. This is another thing that happens. Sounds that are normally no big deal get to me when I am under "high stress," as Gina calls it. It's summer vacation. What could be stressful about that? But the horrible, terrible thing about anxiety is . . . sometimes it's about nothing at all. My body doesn't need a reason to do what it does. By the time I get to Gina's door and turn the old-fashioned brass knob, I have to swallow and swallow to get some spit into my mouth so I can say hello.

"June! Wonderful timing!" Gina says from the corner of the room, where she is using a sticky roller to get all the white hair off her black pants. She rescued a greyhound named Rochester last year. He's not supposed to shed so much, but he has a nervous condition. Go figure.

"I was just asking Alexa to play us some yacht rock."

I have no idea what yacht rock is, but whatever comes over the speaker sounds like the *worst* kind of elevator music. Gina sees me cringe.

"Alexa, STOP," she barks. She has a terrible habit of yelling at Alexa.

"How about you pick us a tune, June. Whatever you're in the mood for," she adds as she settles herself in her big white chair.

I am no fool. I know she's trying to guess my mental state based on what song I pick. She does this sometimes, sneaks in therapy tricks where you'd least expect them. One day she brought in an entire party platter of cheese and chocolate and told me to pick one. When I bit into a square of dark chocolate, she asked, "Why do you think you're feeling more sweet than salty, June?"

I curl into the corner of the cracked leather couch across from her and say, politely, "Alexa, play 'Dog Days Are Over.'" When Florence + the Machine comes on, I nod to the beat. It fills me with purpose again for myself and for this summer. It's a strong female anthem if I ever heard one.

"Ohhh," Gina sighs. "Powerful and punchy, like your hair. It suits you, by the way."

I touch a hand to my head. I'd think she was lying

about it suiting me, but Gina promised she would never lie. She must just have very strange tastes. We sit and listen until Florence fades out. This is another thing I like about Gina. She never hurries.

"Mom shaved hers, too."

"Of course she did. She's team June."

I study Gina's chestnut hair, pulled tightly into a complicated twist. I really hope she does *not* decide to take one for the team.

"So," she asks, grabbing a notepad and clicking her pen, "how has it been since school let out?"

I study the way the light shines through the skylights, creating a maze out of the zigzag pattern on the rug. Truth or silence? There is always a choice with Gina, as long as I don't lie.

I sigh.

"I've assigned myself a fall deadline to fix myself. And I thought getting rid of the hair would do it for me, but it didn't get rid of the thoughts. So now I've still got the worry *and* I look like a baby bird." Tears prick at the corners of my eyes and I blink, blink, *blink* them back into submission before I continue. "And I don't want Mom to be lonely just because Keith left. And some kid recited poetry at me and an old man gave me seeds and I need you to hurry up and make me better."

My mouth is dry as a cotton ball. I stare at the dust particles floating through the sunbeams. Gina clicks her pen.

"Well, that is a tall order," she says finally, but not in a mean way. "And I have three things to say in response."

I look up.

"One," she says, holding up a finger, "I like how you are being proactive about your health, but there's no fixing anxiety. Setting a timeline on it will only add unneeded pressure. You are learning coping skills to help you manage it, and each time you use one of your tools in your toolbox, you get a little bit better at it."

I don't want a toolbox. I want a sledgehammer.

"Two," Gina continues, shifting to tuck both feet under her, "your mother doesn't seem lonely to me. And she would be the first person to tell you that, and—"

"Keith was a loser," I say, "but sometimes he made her laugh and he changed the oil in Thelma and always told Mom she looked nice."

Gina clicks her pen. "Keith was a loser. Period. End of sentence."

He did always look at me like I was contagious and he never offered to do the dishes, so maybe Gina's right.

"Three, June, a boy who recites poetry does not sound so terrible to me." I roll my eyes so hard they actually ache, and she shakes her head. "And the seeds aren't a bad idea. Gardening is often therapeutic. It gets you outside to soak in some vitamin D. It teaches you how to look after something other than yourself. And it gives your hands something to do."

We both look at said hands, which are currently shredding a tissue from the ever-ready Kleenex box on her coffee table. I gather the tiny pieces up off the couch and cradle them.

"I already threw them away," I say. "The seeds."

"Well, keep it in mind. That old man might be onto something." She picks a stray white hair off her lap. "Now, tell me how your breathing exercises are going."

When Gina walks me down the stairs after our session, Mom gives her a paper bag full of her pecan sandies. Gina lights up like a Christmas tree. Mom is like that. She can make anybody happy. Not like me. We might have the same hairdo, but that is where the similarities end.

When we step out into the morning heat, it's almost nine thirty. Thelma shudders in despair as Mom pumps the gas pedal to get her going. But we cannot be late to the library. The Tandy does not need another reason to aim her beady eyes at us. Mom should have brought an extra bag of pecan sandies for her. Except the Tandy doesn't eat desserts. She probably doesn't eat anything at all. She lives off the suffering of others.

5

Accidental Friends

IT IS FOUR FORTY-FIVE P.M. ON THE SIXTH DAY OF summer that I have spent at the library, and I have one small success to report: I have taken over a new hiding place from the Tandy. The nonfiction section. I found a table that is both under an air-conditioning vent and bathed in sun—the perfect combination. I'm by the *T*s. No one has passed my way in half an hour, so I've had plenty of time to practice my house of cards. House building takes steady hands. I can only do it when I'm calm. It is a rare pleasure. I'm just completing the fourth level when—

"Hola, June!"

My hand jerks and the house tumbles.

"Oh, hi, Luis."

Luis sits down across from me. When he squints in the sun from the window, laugh and smile lines transform his face into a map of good cheer. He smells like sun-warmed grass. It's hard not to like Luis.

He sets a stack of books in front of him. All from the *T*s.

"What have you got there?" I say, tipping my head sideways to read the titles.

"Mother Teresa!" Luis says, clapping his sun-spotted hands together.

"The nun lady?" I ask as he turns a giant glossy biography with her face on the front toward me. She is tanned and wrinkly and smiling. She looks a lot like Luis.

"She was not just a nun, June. She is the saint of Calcutta! The protector of the poor and the powerless. She helped so many people. I pray to Saint Teresa. I pray for her to make me useful in my old age." Luis stops and wipes at the corner of his eye.

Oh boy. I am not wired to handle other people's emotions. I begin to straighten my cards, looking *only* at the cards and not the man sniffling behind a pile of Saint Teresa books. Thankfully, we are interrupted.

"You," booms a tall woman barreling between the rows of *T*s like a linebacker. She points a finger. I glance around like, *Who, me?* and sink lower in my chair.

"I need a body," she bellows in a deep, gravelly voice. Her hair is a mass of dark curls with white streaks. She looks like she's been electrocuted and she's not happy about it. Across from me, Luis holds up Mother Teresa like a shield.

"You too," she growls, and points to him.

We look at each other. We do not move. I wish for the Tandy to appear and the two library monsters to destroy each other and leave the kingdom in peace.

"Well?" the tall woman says, snapping her fingers. "Your mother's already in there, and I need all the bodies I can get in Conference Room C."

At the mention of Mom, my knees unlock. If Mom sent her, then as scary as this woman seems, she's passed the test. She's a safe person. I stand and follow. She marches ten paces ahead in her Birkenstocks.

"Where are we going?" Luis whispers to me, a little out of breath. I take the Teresas from under his arm.

"Conference Room C, I guess," I whisper back, and follow the woman, who has *still* not introduced herself, through the rows of books until we cross the large open area by the front desk and enter the meeting room across from the bathrooms.

I spot Mom inside, bent over double and wrestling with the legs of a round card table.

"Need help?"

"Junebug! Good!" She stands and gestures at the tables. "I sent Nicole to find you. Someone forgot to set these up for the poker seminar, and it starts in ten minutes."

So she has a name: Nicole. Seems too soft and fuzzy for a woman who looks like she's ready to arm wrestle. I grab the edge of the table leaning against Mom's side and together we pull the legs like a giant wishbone. Luis starts to sit down.

"Uh-uh. If I can do it, you can too, old man," Nicole says, snapping her fingers again. "I need those chairs unfolded, six per table."

Luis looks from Mom to me before standing. He begins to roll up the cuffs of his shirt.

"Luis Silva, at your service."

"Nicole. But everybody calls me Nix." She towers over Luis, but he gives her the same grin he gives everyone and shuffles off to gather chairs.

Even in the breeze of the air-conditioning, I am sweating. It's good. The more my body moves, the calmer my mind stays. We get all the tables and chairs set up with one minute to spare. Just in time for forty old ladies to shuffle into Conference Room C. Up front, Nix takes the microphone like she owns the place, even though she's only a volunteer. My stomach flip-flops just watching her. I could never do that, stand up and speak in front of a crowd. Give me a thousand stubborn-legged tables any day.

"All right, ladies, we're learning the basics. Pick a spot, but don't get cozy. It'll be round-robin every twenty minutes from here on out!" She gives Mom and me and Luis a terse nod, which I guess is her *thank you and scram.*

I carry Luis's books to the checkout counter for him.

He seems winded but happy as he waves goodbye. By the time I get upstairs to the teen room, Mom is already back at her desk, her yellow sundress glowing in the twinkle lights. A crowd of boys in black T-shirts and skinny jeans stand near her, pretending to browse the graphic novel section. They are not talking to her, just revolving around her like lonely planets. Even without hair, Mom draws people in.

"Junebug! Look who I found," she says with an easy smile that makes one of them laugh nervously. I follow her gaze. There he is, the boy I had managed to avoid for five whole days while also secretly wishing I'd see him, hunched over the chessboard in the far corner. As if I'd poked him with my stare, Homer looks up and grins.

Mom tips her head in his direction, beaming *be friendly* vibes at me.

I sigh, loud and long, and then take my time crossing the room. I am careful not to step on the wishing rug. It seems like bad juju, as my grandparents back in New Orleans would say, to get caught wishing for someone to disappear.

"What are you doing here?" I ask with my back to Mom.

"Nice to see you, too." He leans back in his chair. When I don't say anything, he adds, "If you really want to know, I'm hiding from my sisters."

I take a seat opposite him, because I am tired from all

the table-moving, *not* because I want to "be friendly."

"Where are they?" I ask as Homer studies the chess-board.

"Kat, my older sister, is helping Lucy, my little sister, pick out every single unicorn book in the kids' section."

"You have two sisters?" I can't imagine having siblings. Our house is so quiet. Except for the thoughts in my head.

He nods, moving a knight all the way across the board, which is totally illegal chess. And I would know. I learned to play when I was six. The black-and-white grid, the rules that every single piece has to obey, the way you have to think five steps ahead—chess is one of the few things that makes sense.

"You can't do that, you know," I say, and grab his hand before he can finish jumping his bishop over the knight. His hand is warm and twice the size of mine. I pull back. Unless it's Mom, I do not voluntarily touch people.

"'From childhood's hour I have not been/As other were—I have not seen/As others saw,'" he singsongs, jumping the bishop anyway.

"What does *that* mean?"

"It's Edgar Allan Poe," he says. Then he laughs. "It means I have no idea how to play chess."

I watch him as he rearranges all the white pieces into a triangle.

"You really like poetry, huh?" I say, and sit on my hands to keep myself from putting the pieces back where they belong.

"I like the rhythm," he says, and shrugs, his cheeks turning a little pink.

I think about the music I like, the booming beats that make my heart thump in a good way. I get it. There's a comfort to it. But I don't go around *quoting* it at people.

I cross my arms. "Why are you hiding from your sisters?"

"Because Kat's home from college, and she's even louder than she was the last time I saw her. And see this?" He holds up a tiny orange butterfly clip. "I found this in my hair after breakfast. Lucy." He tucks it back into his pocket. I remember the blue seashell clips I got for Christmas that I can't use now, and my arms and legs get heavy with sadness.

"Homer!" someone squeals, and darts across the wishing well. She takes a flying leap and lands in Homer's lap. The skirts of her Princess Elsa dress settle on them both like a blanket.

"Kitty Kat let me check out *eleven* books," she says before swiveling toward me and staring at my head. "Do you have cancer?"

"Lucy!" Homer says, jumping up so that she falls onto the floor with a thump.

I hold real still, swallowing and swallowing, but the panic rises like the tide. I can feel it in my throat, choking me. My fingers twitch to pull the hair that isn't there.

"What?" Lucy says, whipping her head back and forth from me to Homer, who is suddenly very busy putting all the chess pieces back in order.

Then he looks me right in the eye, even though he's talking to his sister. "Shaved heads are for super-heroes," he says.

Lucy's eyes go wide. "I want to do it!"

He's being nice. But it's no good. The world's tipping and there's nothing to stop me from sliding off the edge. I scoot back from the chessboard. I can fool almost anyone for up to three minutes. That's one hundred eighty seconds. After one hundred eighty seconds, people start to notice the sweat, or my shaking hands, or how my eyes can't focus. I figure I have about thirty more seconds before it all goes sideways.

"There you are!" a voice yells from the doorway. I jump, catching my hip on the Ultimate Survivor display. Copies of *The Hunger Games* and *Divergent* go sliding off the table and spill onto the wishing rug.

"*Homer Juarez*, Mom called twenty minutes ago. We have to get home."

"Chill, Kat. I'm learning chess," Homer says to the

dark-haired girl in the doorway, who is pulling on her sunglasses and already turning away. He takes his time putting the chess pieces off to the side and pushing his chair all the way up to the table. Why is he moving so slowly?! Fifteen seconds. I've got maybe fifteen seconds. Homer *finally* starts to walk away, but as he passes me, with Lucy trailing behind, he stops. And then he *kneels* at my feet. Ten seconds. I can feel the sweat under my arms seeping out onto my T-shirt. He starts to stack the books I toppled over. Why is he doing that? *Why?*

I knock his hand away.

"I got it," I say.

He stands. But he still doesn't leave. I can feel Mom watching us from across the room.

Five seconds.

Go.

Lucy finally tugs the pocket of Homer's cargo shorts, and that gets him moving. She salutes me on her way out and Homer smiles, but I can't make my face move.

When they are finally gone, I slump against the display table, knocking the rest of the books down. Mom comes around her desk and puts a hand on my shoulder, but I shrug it off.

"What was that all about?" she asks, looking toward the door.

"Nothing. It was . . . nothing." I wrap my arms around myself and feel the stickiness of the sweat as it dries. I can shave my head and pretend this summer will be different, but I'm still just a mouse.

6

Friends Forever

GINA PUT ME ON A NEW MEDICINE LAST WEEK. THIS one is so little, I catch myself fishing around for it with my tongue to make sure it's really in there before I swallow. It's yellow and round. Sunshine in a childproof bottle.

It's been almost three weeks since the Homer-Lucy incident, and despite the fact that I have been sleeping better, I am still getting the middle-of-the-day, for-no-reason panic attacks. Last Wednesday, when I couldn't remember if I had returned the knitting book, which I had never "officially" checked out in the first place, I hid under Mom's desk and couldn't stop crying. She had to drive me home on her lunch break so I could look for it. I turned my bedroom inside out and never found it. Then yesterday, I saw it—exactly where it should be in the How-To nonfiction section. I must have put it back after all.

According to Gina, this new little pill is supposed to "buy me time." It won't calm the storm, but it will hold it back long enough for me to do my counting and breathing and "big-picturing," as Gina puts it. That's where I am supposed to think past the super-duper intense moment that has my vision tunneling (missing library book, Lucy's cancer question, Homer's general presence) and instead picture the bologna sandwich I will be eating for lunch in an hour or the Pinkalicious books that need reshelving or Thelma's orange hood baking in the sun and waiting to take us home. "Big-picturing" is anything concrete that gets you beyond the moment so you don't get sucked into a worry loop. The little yellow pill helps me look up.

Except, right now, I am sitting across from Homer and trying to concentrate on our chess match, and I'm finding myself at a disadvantage. After calling me a superhero, Homer started hanging around the teen section every day from eleven to three. It was making me so jittery to see him there doing laps around the room and whistling to himself that I agreed to teach him how to play. I needed something to do with my hands while he was around.

But these pills make me sleeeepyyyyyy. You can't play chess if you can't stay awake. You can't do much of anything, really. This morning I nodded off during Sharika's story time when I was supposed to be passing out egg shakers to the kids. Sharika poked me in the ribs with her Peppa the Pig puppet. She whispered, "Girl, you better get shaking, and I mean that *literally*," before dancing her way back up to the front of the room. She shares an apartment with two of her younger sisters, and she bosses me around just like she does them. It's annoying. And nice.

"And so I discovered I could speak to fish. And that they could speak to me. And now I can't even *walk* past a Captain D's."

"Huh?"

Homer shakes his head at me over the chessboard. I have a feeling this is not the first ridiculous thing he's said to get my attention.

"Get in the game, Junie, or I am going to check you in three."

"It's 'checkmate,' and it is almost impossible to win in three moves."

"Not the way you're playing."

He's kidding. Of course he is. But I lean forward and tap my knight. Homer is the worst player in the history of chess. If I lose to him, all the little yellow pills in the world will not make up for it.

I move my knight from f3 to e5 and take his rook.

He groans as if I had actually trampled him with a horse.

"How come white always moves first?" he asks.

"What?"

"White. You said white always goes first in chess."

"Oh. I don't know. That's just the rules."

He raises an eyebrow. Somewhere along the way, he decided I'm a rebel who hates rules and authority and being like everyone else, because of the shaved head, I guess. The other day he actually said, "You like to"—and I quote—"subvert the norm," which would have been impressive if he hadn't added, "with thy hair that is shorn." He has *no idea* how much I wish I was like everybody else.

I watch as he slides his bishop up to c5. His queen is completely exposed. I could take the win and then go nap. Except the bishop is only allowed to move diagonally. I sigh. I am not a rebel. I am the queen of rule followers.

"Homer, that move isn't legal."

He studies the board and scrunches his face before withdrawing his bishop.

"Right. Just testing you."

After watching him stare at his remaining pieces for a solid two minutes without making a move, I cross my legs and force myself to picture the desert. The other tiny hiccup in this new medicine is that it makes me have to pee all the time.

It's better than the last one, which made me dizzy and want to puke. Or the one before that, which gave me headaches and stole my appetite so I did not even want Mom's homemade apple fritters. Those were dark days. Gina says most of the side effects wear off as your body gets used to it. I wouldn't know. I've never taken any of them long enough to see.

Finally I give in and excuse myself, with a blush and a "Do not cheat" before heading down the stairs to the bathrooms.

Having taken care of business for the thirtieth time today, I am just about to exit the stall when I hear the door creak open. I pause. Bathrooms are awkward places. I don't feel like making small talk or doing that thing where you pretend not to see the other person in the mirror while you're washing your hands. I decide to hide until whoever it is leaves.

"Do you *know* who I just saw upstairs in the teen section?" a voice drawls. An electric current sizzles up my arms. I know that voice. It's Allyson Grayson, the soccer star of my elementary school. She is already almost twelve. And tall and blond and soulless.

Very carefully I step up on the toilet, willing my sneakers not to squeak and the automatic flush to remain still and silent.

"No, who?" someone squeals. It's Jasmine, fellow soccer player. They're always together. I spot her hot-pink flip-flops with the sequins through the crack in the door.

"Homer Juarez!"

My stomach shrivels to the size of a raisin and then poof, evaporates. I shimmy all the way to the back of the toilet. They are talking about my Homer. Not that he's *my* Homer, but he *is* a person I know who knows me back. That has to count for something.

"Who?" Jasmine asks, clueless.

"*Homer*. Geez, Jas, get with the program. The forward on Oakwood's team. He's *gorgeous*."

Oakwood Academy is the private school that's so fancy it has actual ivy growing up its walls. And a gate. And a school song. And uniforms. Homer goes to *Oakwood*? But . . . how? How does he have enough money to go to such a fancy school? And since when is he a soccer star? I press my hands to the sides of the stall to keep them still.

"Ohhhhh, let's go look at him again," Jasmine begs.

Allyson laughs.

The door creaks open and shut as they leave. I don't get down. The sunshine pill is not working. I smell bleach and the fake bubblegum scent of soap. I can't breathe.

Homer is a liar.

Why pretend you are nice and equally friendless when you go to Oakwood and play *sports* and people like Allyson and Jasmine "ohhhhh" over you? Why come to the library every day for *hours* and rearrange the pieces on the chessboard into squares and smiley faces and other totally unplayable configurations when you could be out dribbling the ball, or whatever you do in soccer?

I rub the stubble on my head over and over and then start picking at my cuticles. The skin around my thumbs is red and bloody—like raw hamburger meat. Turns out plucking at the skin around my nails is almost as satisfying as pulling my hair. I've been trying to stop, but who cares, right? I can take a million pills and go to a zillion hours of therapy and I'll still be me.

Allyson is the reason I shaved my head.

It was the last day of school, a day that was supposed to be amazing because it meant I'd survived another year.

A girl in my class, Alisha, had brought in a bracelet-making kit to celebrate her summer birthday. The box said FRIENDS FOREVER BRACELETS on it. They were the kind where you get to pick your string color and a charm like a heart or a star or a butterfly. There was even one that actually said FRIENDS FOR-EVER on it, but Alisha took that one to make for who-ever her best friend was that day, I guess. It's the kind of crafty project I'd seen girls do at lunch or after school on the bus, but I'd never done it because . . . who was I going to make it for? Or with? But Alisha brought enough for everyone and passed them out at recess, and without really planning on it, I sat down in the circle of grass behind the slides with almost my whole class, weaving yellow and green strings together. I picked a star charm to put on at the end.

It was actually fun. The sun was out, and having something like this to do with my hands meant I didn't have to make eye contact and it was okay because everyone else was looking down at their bracelets too. I was more than halfway done and it was getting harder to hold the end of the strings. Other girls were taking turns holding each other's, but I didn't have a partner, so I'd pinched the ends between my knees. Except my hair kept getting in the way. It was so long, it fell all the way to my hips. Without even thinking, I swung it over my shoulder.

That's when I heard somebody squeal.

Quick, quick, I shook my hair out! But it was too late. Across the circle in the grass, Allyson was pointing at my head.

"Gross! What *is* that?" she asked, and *every single person* in the circle looked up.

She'd seen the scab.

My heart squeezed so tight it hurt to breathe. I curled my knees all the way up to my chest. It was the day after Keith left. The day after he called me "incurable." There had been a lot of hair-pulling that night. When Mom saw me the next morning, she cried.

And now Allyson was pretending to throw up in her hands.

I got up and ran inside and pretended to read my library book for the rest of recess. Somewhere between the playground and our classroom, I had dropped the friendship bracelet. I told myself it didn't matter. I didn't have anyone to give it to anyway.

The whispers started at lunch.

"June has lice."

"June has bedbugs."

"June is diseased!"

And they grew louder as the day bled on.

I've never known how to act at school—silent when I should speak, speaking when I should be silent, always sweaty and fidgety and running off to hide in the bathroom . . . like I am right now. I use my teeth to pull the last shred of skin away from my thumbnail. It tears all the way around.

That last day of school, as I was getting off the bus at my stop, when I was almost free, Allyson opened her window and yelled, "Have a good summer, Make-A-Wish June," like I was one of those kids people granted wishes to because I had a disease—an *incurable* disease.

I shaved my head the next day.

The toilet flushes when I get up to leave.

I don't cry. Thank you, new pill. But I also don't go back upstairs. Homer will have to find a new chess partner. I picture him sitting across from Allyson and my heart squeezes. *I am a lion. I am a lion. I am a lion.*

I wander into the children's section instead, where Sharika is kneeling over a tarp next to the train table, helping dozens of kids stick seeds into egg cartons filled with dirt. Luis is next to her. He smiles up at me with his crinkly Mother Teresa face, and *that* makes me tear up for no good reason.

"Oh, my! June, what's wrong?" Luis asks. I wipe at my face with the back of my hand and don't answer. Sharika narrows her eyes at me. I know that look.

"The Tandy is going to hate this mess," I say, trying to change the subject.

Sharika hands the rest of the seeds back to Luis and stands up with a grunt. Then she shoves me into the story-time room, which is empty and dark, with the lights off.

"You better talk to me," she says, wagging a finger in my face the way she knows drives me crazy.

"I'm fine."

"Uh-huh." She doesn't move.

"I am. I just . . ."

She's not going to leave this alone. She's sniffed out my sorrow.

"I hate my hair," I say, and start crying for real. It's not a lie. I do hate it. I hate it every time I look in the mirror, which I try not to do, ever. I hate that it itches my neck and the stubble growing in looks darker than before. I hate how it makes people stare and little kids whisper. It wasn't supposed to be like this. It was supposed to set me free.

"Oh, honey," Sharika says, trapping my hands in hers like moths when I start to pick at my fingers. I make myself stay still and not pull away. "I like your look. It's power chic. But you've got to do you, and if that hair is what's making you so sad, we can do something about that."

"We can?" I ask, staring at her pink extensions.

"June, I have four sisters. There's a hair crisis at least once a week. I've got this. Trust me," she says, walking me back out into the bright lights of the children's area, where I spend the rest of the afternoon helping Luis clean up the stray dirt from the nubby carpet. We haul the egg cartons filled with seeds outside, one by one, to give them a drink of water and some sun before we settle them into their new home on the windowsill in the children's section.

"Ahh, June," he says, beaming down at them. "Now is when the magic starts."

I force myself to smile. I don't tell him I threw away the seeds he gave me.

Mom and Sharika have hatched some kind of plan they will not tell me about. So we are zipping out of the library as soon as their shifts are done, when Homer stops me. *Nonononono.*

"Hey," he says. I am silent.

"I beat you in eight moves," he informs me. That chess game was one hour ago, but also a lifetime ago. Everything's different now.

I look toward the exit, waiting for my mom and Sharika to get me out of this, but they've already made it outside. I see them, on the other side of the doors, watching Homer and me like an exhibit at the zoo. When my not speaking becomes obvious, Homer starts shuffling his feet. He is setting off the automatic doors, open close, open close, open close. Waves of heat from outside fight with icy blasts from the air-conditioning.

"Stop that," I say, and he does. These are the first words I have spoken. They are followed by, "What do you want?"

His smile slips, and it is as satisfying as a good yank of hair.

"I just wanted to schedule our next match."

"But why?" It's the question I've wanted to ask all along, ever since the first day he untangled computer cords and quoted Shakespeare, and now Allyson has left me no choice.

He opens his mouth and then closes it again. It's the first time I've ever seen Homer without something to say.

"Because," he says finally.

"That's it?"

"Because you seemed different, okay?" he adds, looking anywhere but at me.

"You mean I *looked* different." I point to my head and wish my hands weren't shaking. He's just being nice to me because he's bored and I look like something interesting he can tell his friends about later at soccer practice. He doesn't even know the half of how "different" I am.

I start to walk off, but he moves in front of me.

"I didn't mean it that way, June." But the way he says it tells me that's *exactly* what he meant.

I dart around him, but before I'm free, he presses a light blue envelope into my hand and my fingers curl around it automatically.

"Open it later," he mumbles, and walks away, out into the summer afternoon.

The Hair Experience

"OPEN IT! OPEN IT!" MOM AND SHARIKA CHANT from the front seat until I can't stand it another second. Those two are *children* when they get together. I swear it.

We've got all the windows down because Thelma's AC is on the fritz, and the flap of the blue envelope lifts up and down like the wing of a baby bird. I don't want to see what's inside—a letter from a boy I am trying to forget. But here it is and I know my mind will not let it go, a scab to be picked. I slide out the notepaper. It's also blue, and it's thick with gold trim all around the edge, like a wedding invitation. Rich people's stationery. It shouldn't bother me. It's not like we're poor. We rent our house and we have Thelma and we've never gone hungry. But we clip coupons and shop at Goodwill, and there's no way we could ever afford private-school tuition.

I unfold the letter, but before I can make sense of the words, Mom singsongs from the front seat, "You better read that out loud, Junebug. I'm dying of curiosity."

I hold it up and clear my throat, like I'm about to recite a poem. Because that's exactly what it is. Homer Juarez has written me a poem:

On a hot summer morning I met June
Who thinks I am a buffoon
But she taught me to play chess
So she's better than the rest.

Now it's her turn
To eat and to learn
How the Juarezes do it
So let's get to it:

Come over this Friday
For some food and play.
We'll eat, drink, and be merry
And live the night carefree!

Ms. Corinne and Ms. June Delancey are
cordially invited to dinner at the Juarez
residence, 1005 Elderberry Drive, at 7 o'clock
next Friday night. Postscript: Come hungry!

She's better than the rest. What did he mean? Better at chess? Better at computer cord disentanglement?

Better at the silent treatment? And *carefree*? Does he know me at all?

"I knew I liked that boy," Sharika says, and then sighs. "I need to find a man to write me poetry."

Mom studies me in the rearview mirror. She's trying to read me with her eyes, but she doesn't say anything. She'll wait until we're alone. That's how Mom is. Even through the Mr. Exes, she knows what's for other people and what's just between us. Instead she asks Sharika, "What? Andy from the Jiffy Lube didn't write poetry?" That gets Sharika going. She shakes her head and begins to list every single one of the faults of the male species, which carries us all the way to Sawyer Brown Road and a row of shops backing up to the highway.

We park and Thelma sighs, grateful for the break. One of these days she's just going to quit and we will have to find a Thelma 2.0 and I cannot imagine it—a world without her rusty orange comfort. Mom and I follow Sharika into the third shop with the neon-pink sign in the window in the shape of a woman with long, flowing hair.

THE HAIR EXPERIENCE is printed in shiny gold letters on the glass front door. I back up until I am all the way past the sidewalk and in the street. The heat from the road seeps up through my sneakers.

"Uh-uh. No way."

"June, I told you. You have to *trust* me," Sharika

says, clicking her tongue at me in a way that reminds me of the Tandy. Maybe if I tell her that, she'll get so mad she'll want to leave, and I won't have to go into this place that's probably filled with beautiful people like the neon woman on the sign who will stare at me like I'm a stray dog that wandered into the grocery store.

Mom takes off her sunglasses and opens the door. "Junebug, you know I love our look, and my head might be the coolest part of my body now, thanks to you," she says, fanning herself with her glasses like a movie star. "But if you're really unhappy with it, then just give this a shot, hmmm?"

I roll my eyes. I have to. But I'm already following her into the cool white glow of the Hair Experience. I'm still terrified. I don't trust this place. But I do trust Mom.

When I get inside, I realize I had it all wrong from the start. The Hair Experience isn't some fancy, scary beauty salon at all. It's a wig shop! Two of the four walls are lined from top to bottom with mannequin heads of all shapes and colors. And every single one has a different wig on top. It's like Ollivander's wand shop, but with hair!

Sharika leads me over the black-and-white tile floor, which reminds me of a chessboard, then past the salon chairs, where a couple of ladies are getting extensions and scrolling through their phones.

When we get to the heads, Sharika prods me in the shoulder blade.

"Told you I'd take care of you, didn't I?"

I don't say anything, because I can't. There's too much to take in. There are emerald-green bobs and long spiraling curls and blond waves and red layers with bangs. When I reach out to touch a shoulder-length wig with zebra stripes, Sharika grabs it and plops it on my head.

"Go on. Take a look," she orders, grinning and leading me over to a full-length mirror. It's one of those folded mirrors that multiplies you by a million. I stare at an infinity of me's, raise a hand to my striped head . . . and pull it off.

"I like it. But it's not me," I say. Not that I know what "me" *is*.

"Well, take your pick. You've got about a hundred and fifty more."

Sharika fluffs the zebra hair a little and replaces it on the mannequin.

I spend the next hour trying on wig after wig, while Mom and Sharika and even the ladies in the chairs cheer. Mom tries them on too. She finds one that looks exactly like her old hair. It's a deep, dark coffee color that falls in waves down her back. I forgot how pretty Mom's hair was. She catches me studying her in the mirror and whips it off.

"Been there, done that," she says, and plucks a deep burgundy one with a white streak in it off the nearest mannequin.

"Oh, yes," she says, twirling so that the long hair fans out behind her. "That's more like it." She looks like Ariel from *The Little Mermaid*, but tougher.

I need to make up my mind. But nothing feels right. Not the blondish one that is kind of like my real hair or the green curly one or the spiky black one. I walk back and forth, trying to find something I haven't seen yet. When I spot it, up high in the right-hand corner, all I can think is, *There you are.*

It's too high to reach. The owner, a white-haired woman even shorter than me, fetches a stepladder. When Sharika tries to hold on to her elbow to help her up, because she looks like she is *at least* a hundred, she waves her away with a "Don't *fuss.*" She carefully tips it into her fingers and climbs down. Then she turns to me and holds it out with a smile. She nods with approval when I take it from her gently.

I keep my back to the infinity mirror when I place it on my head. My scalp tingles like it's welcoming home an old friend. I am facing the two ladies getting their extensions. When they see me, they put down their phones and clap, and the sound of it fills me up. I do a little curtsy in my shorts and sneakers. I have never felt so beautiful and I haven't even looked yet.

I turn to the mirror but close my eyes at the last second. I'm scared the picture won't match how I feel. It'll be another lie my brain has told me.

Next to me, Mom leans in and whispers, "Junebug, you are stunning. Open your eyes." So I do.

All the me's in the mirror grin. They lift their millions of hands and touch the electric-blue hair. Electric is the word for it. A powerful current begins to hum in my veins. It is a color you can't find in nature. It's the color of blue raspberry suckers and superheroes. The hair is cut at a sharp angle so that the back is shorter than the front. The tips fall in a smooth curve that cups my chin. I pet it. It's softer than I would have guessed. Looking at the new June, I stand up straighter.

Mom puts her hands on my shoulders. She really *is* a superhero in her new red hair. Together, we're a dynamic duo. Standing here in our tank tops and shorts and wigs, we are the fierce females I hoped we'd be on the first day of summer.

Then I check the price.

Two hundred dollars. I whip the wig off like it's on fire and back away from Mom until I bump into the mirror.

"June! What in the world?"

I run up the stepladder to try to get the wig back in place. The longer I touch it, the more I want it. I've got to get it out of my hands. The ladder wobbles and Mom grabs me from behind.

"Sit down!" she cries, and pulls me back so that I

fall into her with the wig still in my hands. I collapse onto the stepladder. No one is clapping now.

"I changed my mind."

"Changed your *mind*? June, I saw how you looked at yourself in that wig. There's no changing your mind. You're getting it."

I flip over the price tag. Mom's smile crumples, just a little, before she can smooth it out again.

"There is no reason you cannot go home as blue as a berry right now." She holds out a hand. "Come on, follow me."

She slips off her own wig and pulls me up. I see what she's doing. She's making a sacrifice. My wig instead of hers.

"No." I jerk to a stop before we can get to the front counter. "Mom, you look like a warrior in that hair. And . . . it's my fault you got rid of your own." The shame of that morning comes rushing back—how I thought I was doing some brave, amazing thing taking that razor to my head—but then it all fell to pieces when I saw myself in the mirror. My cheeks get hot and the black-and-white tiles on the floor blur with the tears I'm holding back.

I hear Sharika and the owner talking softly. I imagine what they're saying. We've wasted their entire afternoon. We mussed up all the wigs. We don't belong here. "Please, Mom," I whisper. "You have got to get it."

She shakes her bald head no.

I shake mine yes.

Then she keeps shaking her head but starts doing this shimmy thing with her shoulders. She's trying to make me laugh. It won't work this time.

Over at the counter, Sharika clears her throat. She and the owner walk toward us.

"Honey," the owner says, low and soft, "do you know what day it is?"

"Wednesday, ma'am," I reply. I am thankful for a question with a straight answer.

"Well, yes." She nods. "And Wednesday happens to be our BOGO day."

I am lost. "What's a *bow-go*?"

"Buy one, get one free, June baby!" Sharika shouts so loud it makes me jump. "Everybody knows that."

The owner winks.

Before either Mom or I can utter a word of protest, she takes the wig and slowly places my new blue hair on my head, smoothing the stray hairs stuck to my cheek.

Over at the counter, I catch Mom shaking her head when Sharika hands her credit card to the cashier. Even with the BOGO, we cannot afford *one* wig on Mom's library salary.

I whisper, "Thank you" to Sharika as Mom and I walk to the door with our new hair and our heads held high. I've never been given a gift like this. I've never been given anything from anyone, other than Mom and my grandparents. When we walk out, the setting sun catching on Mom's new hair, I make a silent promise. Somehow, I'm going to pay Sharika back. Because I'm pretty sure she just changed my life.

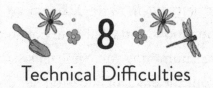

8
Technical Difficulties

THE FOLLOWING WEEK, MOM AND I STAND BEFORE the Tandy for inspection. She stares at our red and blue heads, now that we've finally dared to wear our new hair to Mom's place of business. Her mouth flattens. Her nostrils flare. And then she lets out a sound like a hiss. Mom reaches into her purse and pulls something out. When she opens her fist, the ugly brown-and-orange scarf opens like a flower.

"Thank you for letting me borrow this, but I won't be needing it any longer," Mom says, sweet as pie.

The Tandy crushes it in her talons.

"This is not a *costume* party," she growls. "This is work."

"Yes, I know," Mom replies. "And if that's all, I'd like to get back to it."

Before the Tandy can speak again, we march ourselves up the stairs to the safety of the twinkle lights and wishing rug.

When I put my blue hair on just an hour ago and studied myself in the tiny square of our bathroom mirror, it was like inserting a plug into a socket—I could feel the electricity begin to tingle down my spine. What Mom does not know, and what I am not going to tell her now that she's humming some nonsense song to herself and sorting out the stack of books on her desk, is this: it felt so good, I skipped my meds. Who needs a yellow pill of sunshine when you have electric hair?

Today I'm in charge of tallying the votes on our Who Did it Better: Book or Movie? display. Mom pinned the book covers of *Dumplin'* and *The Fault in Our Stars* and *Eragon* and a bunch of others up on the wall by the window next to their movie posters. Kids are supposed to vote on which is better, the book or the movie. So far the books are killing it. I'm just finishing up my count when the lights flicker.

Right at that moment, like something out of a horror movie, somebody taps me on the shoulder. I yelp and drop my pen and all my color-coded Post-its.

"Sorry!" It's Homer and he looks . . . shy. He's not meeting my eyes, and he's kind of hunched over. In the few weeks I've known him, I've never seen him act like he didn't belong in the center of the room.

"You can't sneak up on a person like that," I say. It comes out too sharp. I picture the blue envelope with his letter inside that's been sitting on my dresser at home for the last week. He wrote, *She's better than the rest*, and I can't even be nice.

"Sorry," he says. Great, now I've got him apologizing to me. "Nice hair."

I touch the soft fringe that hits my chin. "Yeah?"

"Yeah," he says. "I mean, I liked it before, too. You're rebel June both ways."

I don't know what to say to that. I'm not good with compliments. Especially ones I'm not sure are true. A heavy silence falls between us. I know I'm supposed to talk next. That's how conversation goes. But I also can't help remembering what I know about him now after hearing Allyson in the bathroom, and it feels like I'm talking to a stranger.

"Well," I say, holding up my Post-its. "I have to finish this."

"Wait."

He shuffles from foot to foot. "Did you read the poem? Are you and your mom coming to dinner tomorrow?"

"I, uh—"

"Ms. Delancey!" the Tandy barks, stalking through the door like a witch who lost her broom. Homer turns away from me to see what the commotion is about, and for once I am grateful for her terrifying presence. She's followed by a man so tall he has to duck to get through the doorway. He looks like the Man in the Yellow Hat from Curious George, if the Man in the Yellow Hat wore trendy black glasses and carried a laptop. I use the distraction to hurry away from Homer toward Mom's desk.

"We've had a disaster," the Tandy says.

"What's the problem, Betty?" Mom asks, as calm as can be.

I did *not* know the Tandy's first name was Betty. It's so . . . sweet.

The Tandy narrows her eyes at the new set of fantasy novels Mom is labeling.

"You didn't notice the power surge a few moments ago? I know you don't have your library science degree, but you *do* know how to use the computer system, yes?" This is why the Tandy can't keep a full-time librarian around. Too bad a degree doesn't teach you how to be nice.

"I do," Mom replies with a nod, but her mouth quirks up just a teensy bit. She's actually terrible with technology. When Sharika gave Mom her old iPhone, I was the one who set it up. She still doesn't know how to update her apps.

Thankfully, the Tandy is too wrapped up in her "disaster" and barrels on. "It seems that power surge has caused some sort of *malfunction*. We're having to check out books *by hand*." She says "by hand" like she has been asked to bake her own bread from scratch. Which *is* something Mom can do.

"This is Mr. James. He has come to reset the system

and do . . . whatever it is that we pay him to do in crises such as these." The Tandy marches off without so much as a goodbye.

I watch her disappear down the stairs and then scan the room for Homer. He's gone. But the pieces on the chessboard have been rearranged in a not-so-subtle question mark.

When the tall man steps forward, I get a better look at him. What I see sends a shiver up and down my spine so fierce I imagine this is what electrocution feels like. Between the dark hair and blue eyes, all I can see is Nick. Nick, the stuff of nightmares. Literally. One of the reasons I don't sleep is so I never have to ever see that face again.

"Sam," the tall man says, pushing his glasses up his nose with his knuckle and offering a hand for Mom to shake, which she does.

"It's nice to meet you, Sam," Mom says, and stands and smooths her green sundress.

"Same," he says to both of us, and then flips open his laptop. "Now, let's see what the problem is, exactly."

Sam. Not Nick. But still, I can't look at him. I mumble some excuse about Sharika needing me and sprint down the stairs to the children's section. It's not a total lie. I really do want to thank Sharika again for my new hair. When I get down there, she's reading *Miss Rumphius* to a group of kids who came from the day camp down the road for story time.

I lean against a back shelf to listen. I love this story. When Miss Rumphius is a little girl, she dreams of traveling to faraway places, where she can see and do things that she can't see and do in her tiny seaside town. Her grandfather thinks this is a mighty fine plan, but he also tells her to "do something to make the world more beautiful."

It's a nice idea, jumping all over the globe and adventuring like that. It would be what I would wish for if I didn't have anxiety slowing me down like a suitcase with a wobbly wheel. Books help ease the trapped feeling. At least I can adventure with Miss Rumphius and travel through a wrinkle in time with the Murrys and live in a bus with Coyote Sunrise and run a motel with Mia Tang and drink the moon with Luna. Mom always says, if you've got a book, you can go anywhere.

In the story, Miss Rumphius grows up and does exactly what she planned. She moves far away, and she works in a library and climbs mountains and rides camels and drinks straight from a coconut. When my second-grade teacher read the book to us, I came home from school and told Mom all about the coconut. And she went out and found one! She cracked it with a hammer right over our kitchen sink. It wasn't half as sweet as I'd imagined. But I didn't mind, because now I knew what a real coconut tasted like.

Sharika's at the part now when Miss Rumphius is

old and moves back to her seaside town. She starts a little garden, thinking it would be a nice thing for an old lady to do. But it turns out her garden doesn't want to be little. The flowers have a mind of their own. They spread over the hillside and along the village roads, and soon the whole town is covered in blue and purple and pink flowers! As Miss Rumphius keeps finding her flowers everywhere she goes, she realizes she did the thing her grandfather asked. She has made the world a more beautiful place.

The way Sharika reads it, I can hear the sound of the waves and taste the coconut and brush my fingers along the feathery tips of the flowers. By the time she finishes, all the kids are begging to water the little seedlings on the windowsill. Sharika spots me as she is closing the book and waves me over to help. Thanks to Luis, the seedlings are almost plants now, with pale green leaves. I touch each one and wish for it to grow grow grow! Miss Rumphius would be proud.

When the campers leave to have a snack outside, I sort through the few seedlings that didn't make it. Some sure tried. One is almost as tall as the rest, but it's yellow instead of green and already curling up into itself. I snip its egg cup free from the rest with the pair of scissors we keep on a hook behind the desk, out of reach of the kids. I should throw it away. It's obviously not going to make it. It doesn't look like the others—too limp and floppy and all the wrong color. But I can't dump it in the garbage with the checkout receipts and gum wrappers. It's not dead yet. You don't give up on something if it's still got some fight in it.

Except now that I have it in my hand, I don't know what to do with it. I carry it over to the window to get some sunshine. We sit together, the plant and me, until I hear the announcement for the poker seminar. It has become so popular, Nix upped the frequency of meetings. She's here almost every afternoon. Mom heard from Sharika, who heard from the special collections librarian, that Nix lost her husband to cancer a few years back, just like Luis lost his wife. I guess the library is full of lonely people.

After I thank Sharika one more time for my new hair, I sprint up to the teen section to deposit my seedling and pick up the petit fours Mom brought. She takes orders whenever she can to bring in extra money, but the baby shower she made these for got canceled when the mother-to-be went into labor the night before. So now we're up to our elbows in tiny white cakes with pink rattles on them. I've been eating the lemon-filled ones for breakfast and I am not complaining.

When I get upstairs, Sam is *still* here. I know the computers are fixed because the line of people waiting to check out downstairs is back to normal. So why is he hanging around? I know he's not Nick, but the sight of him puts me on edge. I want him *gone*. He's so busy tapping away at Mom's purple iPhone that neither one notices me standing right behind them. When I clear my throat, Mom jumps.

"Poker's starting," I say, and nudge her with my knee so I can crawl under the desk and get the Tupperware container of petit fours. While I'm down there, I hide my seedling in the corner to bring home later and then scramble out.

"Here you go. All updated," Sam says, and hands Mom her phone.

Mom smiles and thanks him. I don't like the way she's looking at him one bit. That is *not* the look of a strong, independent woman.

"I could have done that," I say, cradling the box and moving between them.

"It was no problem," Sam says without taking his eyes off Mom.

"It would have been 'no problem' for me either."

"June!" Mom says, half laughing, even though there's nothing funny.

Sam's phone buzzes. It's on a clip on his belt. He checks it and sighs. "Looks like I've got another service call to make."

"Exit's that way," I say, and nod my blue head toward the stairs.

"Nice to meet you both," he says, turning his too-blue

eyes on each of us in turn. I watch Mom carefully, the way her head dips when she smiles. She did that with Keith. And she did it with terrible Nick, who we left New Orleans for and who I will not let myself think about. I don't remember her with my father, another chef-in-training she met at her cooking school, because he was never in the picture, but I'm sure it was the same. This was *not* the plan. I watch Sam disappear down the stairs and pray on the wishing rug that's the last we see of him.

I am late to poker. But Luis managed to set up the tables and chairs all by himself. He is now sitting *in* one of those chairs, waiting for Nix to finish the introduction. I crouch down beside him.

"You play poker now?" I whisper.

"Sí. Yes. Nicole is teaching me," he says, pointing to where she's shouting orders into the microphone. He is watching Nix like she's announcing the Oscars. What is *with* everybody today?

Soon the room fills with the whirring sound of shuffling cards, and Nix marches over and points a finger at me. She's always pointing a finger at me. "You're late. Luis and I had to get this room game-ready without you."

"I didn't mind," Luis says dreamily. I look down to keep my eyes from rolling.

"I brought food," I offer, and hold up the Tupperware.

Nix sets it on the table and unsnaps the lid. All business. Then she takes her time selecting one of the little white cakes and lifts it up to inspect the bottom. Mom's the only one I have ever seen do that. She says a petit four should be as neat underneath as it is on top.

After her examination, Nix takes a bite. She closes her eyes and chews slowly. Then she holds it up to study the neat layers of red jam and white cake and cream filling. She got a strawberry one. "Perfect." Nix *would* think she knows everything about everything.

"*You* made these?" she asks, and I want to say yes just to wipe that surprised look off her face. But I shake my head instead.

"My mom did."

"Well. Isn't that interesting," she says, except she doesn't sound interested at all. Instead she's already leaning toward the closest table.

"Diane, you have a full house and you just folded. Do you even listen to me when I talk, or are you too busy playing solitaire on your phone?" she says, moving away from us. But not before she swipes the entire box of petit fours without even a thank-you.

Next to me, Luis grins and sighs.

9

The ABCs of Gardening

THE JUAREZ DINNER IS NINE HOURS AND FOURTEEN
minutes away and I still haven't given Homer an answer.
I lean against Thelma's window as we rumble along the
road, and she rattles my head like she's trying to knock
some sense into me. Mom already tried. Last night she
made my favorite fried avocado BLTs and then gave me
her version of "a talking-to."

"Junebug," she said, wiping a smoosh of green from
the corner of her mouth, "you know it's you and me for
life, right?"

I nodded. I had seen where this was going when I
spotted her homemade aioli. It's her special-occasion
sauce to win people over. It's really just fancy mayonnaise.

"We do all right, the two of us, yeah?"

I nodded again, making sure the bread slices on my
sandwich were in perfect alignment so I didn't have to
look at her.

"But sometimes you have to open yourself up to more than what you've got to know what you're missing. And that can be scary—for anybody," she added. She sounded like Gina. I wondered if the two of them had talked this out before dinner. Mom's not great with the inspirational speeches. She's more of a doer than a talker. This was as far as I'd ever seen her go into the feelings talk. She looked about as uncomfortable as I did. "Do you understand what I'm saying?"

"No?" It came out like a question. Because I really didn't. I just crossed my fingers that this wasn't her way of telling me she was going to date Sam, because we would *for sure* be getting into some feelings talk about that.

She took a long sip of iced tea before putting both her elbows on the table like she was getting down to business. "I think we should accept Homer's invitation."

I choked on my sandwich. I had just had the most awkward conversation of my life with him before Sam showed up. Dinner with his whole family in a place I couldn't escape would be torture.

"I . . . can't," was all I said, and when Mom didn't say anything back, I figured she'd dropped it. She pushes, but she never pushes too hard. But as we passed each other in the hall on our way to sleep, she whispered along with her good nights, "I made a watermelon pie just in case."

And now it is nine hours and *three* minutes until this dinner and I still haven't officially told Homer no, because, well, that would involve talking to him. The panic is starting to creep in. I've moved on from tearing at the skin around my thumbs to my index fingers. I don't know what I'm going to do when I run out of digits.

When Mom screeches to a halt in the library parking lot (we are predictably late), I struggle with Thelma's door handle because my fingers are shaky. And when the glass doors slide open to welcome us into the cool of the library, I start gulping like a fish out of water.

I don't know what to do. And that's a problem. Because if my mind cannot settle on a solution, it won't leave me alone. It picks and picks at the "what-ifs" until I am oozing with worry. It's the missed prayers all over again. I said them hundreds of times, because my brain couldn't decide when was enough, and so . . . it was never enough. This was after Nick left, after "the incident." I wish I had my yellow seedling with me. Last night I set it right next to my head on the bedside table, and just knowing it was there helped me go to sleep.

I find a corner in the nonfiction section and sink to the floor. Life should be like Mom's baking. Follow the recipe perfectly and you create perfection. Or like chess. Memorize the rules and the moves and practice enough and you can beat anybody. But it feels more like my yellow plant. There's no reason why it didn't grow like the rest and this morning it looked even weaker and yellower than before. Sometimes you can do everything right and it's still not enough.

Around noon, I crawl out from my hiding place to fish through the recent returns cart. Someone brought back a tattered copy of *The ABCs of Gardening*, and it feels lucky, like I'm meant to have it so I can care for my plant. But then Homer walks up and my luck runs out. While I am looking anywhere but at his face, I spy a pink glittery barrette that I bet Lucy stuck behind his ear. I'm 90 percent sure he doesn't know it's there, and I will not tell him because I don't want to "open a dialogue," as Gina says. I want this dialogue shut down fast.

I risk a glance at his face and he's smiling, just like he always is, but he's not really looking at me either and now this is the second awkward meeting we have had in less than twenty-four hours. My nervous heart can't keep this up.

I tuck my new hair behind my ear and then do it again and again and again until I have to grip my *ABCs* book with both hands to stop.

"Hi, June," he says eventually, after he realizes *I'm* not going to say hello. He shifts from foot to foot in his Adidas sandals.

"Hello," I say to his feet, because I can't look at his face again.

"I, uh, like your hair," he says. I don't know what to say, so I say nothing. After a torturous pause he asks, "Hot outside, huh?" I know we are in trouble when all we have to talk about is the weather.

I clear my throat.

He clears his.

His feet stop shuffling.

I feel the moment slipping away. Right here in recent returns is where I will say goodbye to my almost friend. It's relief and it's pain. I don't know why life can't ever be just one thing. It's confusing and it hurts. I remind myself that this is what I wanted. I start to back away, shaking my head. I hope that's enough for him to get the message and for us to go back to being strangers.

"There you are!" Sharika shouts from behind us. I jump and pivot, my heartbeat loud in my ears. She is breathless and frantic and I've never seen her that way before. Nothing ruffles Sharika. She is unrufflable.

"What's the matter?" I ask, not only because I'm dying to know but because it gives me a reason to stay turned away from Homer.

"Mrs. Tandy's on the warpath," Sharika whispers. "Some of the egg cartons are leaking. Apparently, there's some water damage to the windowsill next to the story-time room."

"So we'll move them," I say, walking away from Homer and toward the children's section.

Sharika shakes her head. "It's too late. She's dumping them in the trash. In *front* of the kids."

I break into a run and Sharika follows at a swift march. Homer zooms by us both, taking the corner past the Captain Underpants display at high speed. But it doesn't matter. When we get there, the Tandy is dusting her hands over a supersized Hefty bag. The windowsill is empty except for a few crumbles of dirt. A group of little kids from the day camp stands a few feet back, crying and hugging one another.

"What have you done?" I yell. I've never raised my voice to an adult. But Tandy is *killing* the plants in front of *children*, just like she snaps when they touch a book with sticky hands or clicks her fingers at my mom when we are one second late. I can't take it anymore! Right now I am not mousy June. I am June the *lion*.

The Tandy flattens her mouth into a line as thin as a pin. "Do not raise your voice in my library."

"It's not *your* library! It's everybody's library!" I shout even louder.

She dismisses me with a wave.

"This pet project of yours," she says to Sharika, "will cost the library hundreds of dollars in damages. If that windowsill has to be replaced, it will be coming out of *your* paycheck."

Sharika mumbles an "okay." Sharika has never mumbled anything in her life. She is loud and sure, and the fact that the Tandy is making her act this way makes me want to spit. Sharika might be a little better off than me and Mom, but she does *not* have hundreds of dollars to give to the Tandy. I swore when she bought me my wig that I would pay her back. Maybe this is the universe's way of giving me the chance. Not with money, because obviously I don't have any, but with something else. I think I might have the beginning of an idea. I keep my mouth shut tight, though, and let the Tandy finish, because this is going to have to be a super top secret mission.

"Dirt and filth," she's saying now, "have no place in this library." She points to her Hefty bag. "These are in the trash where they belong."

She turns her beady stare on Homer.

"Young man, take these to the dumpster ASAP. And no more special projects, Ms. Jones. The books themselves should be quite enough entertainment, don't you think?"

Sharika mutters, "Okay," and we watch as the Tandy marches back toward her lair in the sorting room.

When she's out of sight, Sharika steers the children to her desk to wipe tears and pass around the bowl of stickers and temporary tattoos.

I survey the wreckage. Little clots of soil dot the windowsill, but other than that, I can't see *any* water damage. The Tandy has been circling our plants and clucking her tongue for weeks. This was just her excuse to get rid of them.

I turn to find Homer gathering the yellow strings of the garbage bag, but I touch his hand to stop him before he can knot it. It is the fourth time we have touched. The first was on the day we met, when he handed me the knotted computer cord. The second time I grabbed his hand to block an illegal chess move. Then I knocked his arm away from the stack of fallen books after he called me a superhero. This is the first time, however, that I've actually touched him out of niceness and for longer than a millisecond. My heart's thumping like crazy, but I don't hate it.

"Come with me," I say. "And bring the bag." His face breaks out in a huge grin, and it's like the old Homer is back and before I can stop myself, I smile too. Maybe my blue hair *is* good luck.

We find Luis in the biographies, reading up on Mother Teresa again and waiting for Nix to arrive for poker.

"Luis, you know all about plants, right?" I ask.

"Sí. Though 'all' is a big word. My wife and I, we had a little farm. It was not much and our sons run it now, but yes, I know plants."

"Do you still have some of your gardening tools around? The ones you used to put the zenas at the bus stop?"

"The zinnias? Yes. I keep the tools in my car. In case of emergencies."

I cannot imagine what a plant emergency would be. Except, I guess that's what we're having now.

"Well, this is a 9-1-1 plant emergency," I say, and Homer nods. "Can we borrow your tools?"

He closes his book and stands. "I will help."

At one o'clock on this last Friday in June, the air is not just hot, it's a wet blanket of air that settles on your shoulders and wraps itself around your middle until every breath feels like you're being squeezed like a sponge. It's the kind of heat that cooks eggs on sidewalks and melts bicycle tires. But when Homer and I follow Luis out to his blue hatchback, I'm not worried about the heat. I'm not worried about anything but my plants.

Luis opens the back and we lean away to let the trapped hotness escape. He hands me the pointy tool that I once thought was a knife, but that I now remember is a spade. And then he carefully lays out gloves; a three-pronged thing that looks like a tiny pitchfork, which he explains is a cultivator; and a full-length shovel, which I don't know how he fit in his tiny car.

"That should do it," I say, even though I have no idea what "it" is exactly. I'm winging it. I have never *winged* anything in my life. "Come on."

I lead them both down the sidewalk behind the library, past the dumpster where the Hefty bag is *supposed* to go, and down a grassy hill. It ends in a row of tall, shady trees that back up to the river. This river winds itself all through our small town. You think you're miles away from it and then you come upon a turn in the road and there it is, muddy and brown and wide and waiting for canoers and kayakers and picnickers. I like knowing it's here, running swift and hidden just around the bend.

"This is still library property?" Luis asks, shading his eyes to glance back up the hill at the brick building.

"Yeah, but no one ever comes down here," I say. This is another one of those secret things, like the magic of the recent returns shelf, that I figured out after spending so many hours at the library.

"June, I am not so sure this is a good idea." Luis twists the gloves in his hands.

"But you planted your zinnias by the bus stop."

"Yes, but I had permission and I am an old man. People tend to forgive us our quirks."

"Well, I have a few quirks of my own." I jam my spade in the ground to test how hard the soil is. It sinks easily enough. The river has made the dirt softer here. "Surely," I add, "Mother Teresa wouldn't argue with *saving the lives* of innocent plants." I don't feel great about calling on his love for the saint to do something that may not be totally okay. But I owe it to Sharika to save her seedlings.

When Luis starts to walk away, my heart drops. The one time I try to do something big and brave for someone else and it flops. Then he holds up his hand and waves us forward.

"Come on, you two. We must find a break in these trees to plant. These babies need a lot of sun."

"Thank you, thank you, thank you, Luis!" I shout, and Homer and I run to catch up with him. Luis stops at a little open spot, out of sight of the library entrance, but still close enough that I can spot Thelma's orange hood in the parking lot.

"*Rudbeckia hirta*," Luis says, passing out the gloves.

"Rude *what*?" Homer asks.

"*Rudbeckia hirta*," Luis repeats happily, all the guilt of trespassing gone. He pokes the dirt over and over again with the cultivator. "That is the name for these flowers. Also known as black-eyed Susans. When they bloom, they will be bright yellow with dark centers. Very pretty, like little suns, and the butterflies love them."

Luis shows us how to break up the soil with the cultivator and the spade. He took away the shovel after I almost stabbed my own toe with it.

"You have to make the ground soft and loose. See?" He brushes his hand over the top layer of dirt like he's playing in the sand. "Then you have to plant the little ones about a foot and a half apart from each other. The roots, they need room to wiggle," he says, wagging his fingers in the air. A clot of dirt lands on his head.

Homer snorts, which starts a tickle in my throat. Soon we're both laughing so hard it's shaking drops of sweat from my nose.

Luis clicks his tongue. "First you need my help. Then you laugh. I am going up to the library to cool off and fetch the watering can."

We both try to stop then. We really do. But it's impossible when he gets up with a groan and the dirt slides forward into his bushy eyebrows.

He swipes at it and points to us. "You remember how much you need me while I am gone, yes?"

"Yes," we both say, and salute him.

After he disappears over the hill, I kneel in the soft dirt, so much cooler than the air, and Homer kneels next to me. We lay the wrecked plants out on the ground, sifting through whatever we can save. It isn't much. The Tandy tore so many of them to pieces. It hurts to look at their shredded leaves and snapped buds. We gather what's left and line them up next to what will be their new home.

I watch Homer carefully untangle one green stem from another and set them down in their places like dolls. He's so gentle and patient, like he was with the computer cords. It doesn't fit with the picture of him as some superrich, supercool soccer star. It's like he's two people at once. I want to know which one is real. And I'm finally feeling gutsy enough to ask.

"When you said I was different," I say, and dig my fingers into the dirt, "did you mean different bad or different good?" My heart is louder than the birds, louder than the buzzing bees, louder than the river rushing by. Right now it's the loudest thing on the planet.

He looks up at me. "My dad says there's no good or bad. Just different."

"That's not an answer."

Homer sits back on his heels and looks down at the plant he's cradling like a baby, but he doesn't speak. And he keeps *not speaking*, until I feel like I'm going to drown in the silence.

"Why do you want to be friends with me, Homer? We barely know each other."

When he still doesn't talk, I wipe my hands on my shorts. When I get up, the blue tips of my new hair brush against my cheeks. I can't keep doing this *back-and-forth, maybe friends, maybe not* thing. I don't have enough people in my life not to care whether they come or go. I turn my back to him and start walking up the hill. But it's slow going because my legs are heavy.

"You're the first person I ever said a line of poetry to," he calls out.

"B-but . . . ," I sputter, and turn. "Half your sentences are quotes."

He shrugs. "To you, maybe. But at my school, people kind of know me for only one thing . . . and it's not poetry."

Soccer, I think, but don't say because I'm still not supposed to know that.

"But I love it," he confesses. "I love the way the lines make word pictures, and every poem is like a photograph that's bright and sharp." Homer's whole body lights up as he talks. "I guess when I saw your hair, I figured I'd try out the whole poetry thing on somebody who seemed like they didn't care what other people thought."

Me, someone who doesn't care what people think, ha! He doesn't know me at all. He just likes an idea of me and it's not even a true one. It will all come out eventually, though—the minute he sees me panic or finds me hiding under Mom's desk or yanking skin off my fingers.

"I—"

"You know," Homer says, talking over me because he's excited now. "In a weird, backward-universe kind of way, you probably know the real me more than the kids I've been at school with for the last six years." He looks up at me and grins, and even though I know better, I want more than anything for it to be true. Before I can think another second about it, I say, "Fine," and sit back down next to him in the dirt.

"Fine what?"

"Fine, my mother and I would love to come to your house tonight for dinner."

"For real?"

"Yeah. But unless you want us both to miss it, we better get to work."

We move in silence after that, but it's an easy silence, not like before.

When we are done rescuing all the plants that can be rescued, I lean back against a tree, feeling the grit that has found its way up and over my flip-flops and in between my toes. Homer steps out of the sun and into the shade next to me. We survey our handiwork—four neat lines of green, already drinking up the water from the river and the earth.

"'Why, who makes much of a miracle?'" Homer says. "'As to me, I know of nothing else but miracles.'"

"Is that another one of your poems?" I ask.

"Walt Whitman's," he answers, "but he let me borrow it."

Watermelon Pie

I THINK ABOUT WALT WHITMAN'S POEM AS THE DIRT swirls down the shower drain in clumps and Mom yells from the kitchen that we're going to be late for the Juarezes if I don't hurry up. Is that how Homer sees it? The world full of miracles like pennies in a fountain?

I scrub my head, feeling the burr of hair that is coming in darker than before. My world is not a place of miracles. At least it hasn't been. My world is full of dark corners and the anxious thoughts that skitter there. There are people who have made it better. And there are people who have made it so much worse. I pick at the dirt under my nails. The soap stings the edges of my bloody cuticles. Just for a second, I let myself think of "the incident."

I was eight and it was summer. I didn't know it would be the last time I would see Nick, Mom's second boyfriend, the whole reason we left New Orleans and moved up here. After three years of us eating the red-sticker food at Kroger and Mom answering phones at a music store just so she could get an employee discount for his equipment, Nick *finally* signed with a record company down on Music Row. He was all set to make it big.

Mom cooked a fancy meal to celebrate—crawfish étouffée and red beans and rice and crispy fried okra set out on a white linen tablecloth we never had a reason to use before. She was blowtorching the crème brûlées when we heard the jingling bells of the ice cream truck.

Nick was relaxed, not like he usually was. He was always worked up about something—some guy in his band wanted the lead in a song, but only *Nick* was allowed to write the songs, or some music producer came to a show but left in the middle, or he saw a $500 pair of jeans he was *sure* Keith Urban wore and couldn't understand why Mom didn't want him to get them. It didn't take much. I had learned to watch for the veins on his neck. If they stood out, I stayed away. But today he was leaning back in his chair so only the back two legs touched. And he smiled at me, so I smiled back. I was wearing my favorite purple sundress with the butterflies on it and I was happy.

The ice cream truck circled back around the block and this time the sounds were louder, which meant it was close! I scooted back from the table. I had four dollars and a quarter saved up. If I ran now, I could catch it.

I wanted one of those firecracker Popsicles that turned your tongue red, then blue.

Nick's chair snapped down with a thwack. He grabbed my wrist. "Your mama made dessert," he hissed. "Sit back down at the table." I knew better than to disobey. But I wanted that Popsicle so bad I could taste it.

I twisted. But he wouldn't let go. And then my wrist started to hurt. He had those strong fingers from guitar. I twisted harder, but he held on tighter than before. That's when my heart started beating real fast. Would he ever let go? I pictured my arm snapping right off, like a Barbie doll. And that's when I really panicked. I was so scared I started to whimper. "Hush," he whispered, and jerked me hard, and that's when I felt something in my shoulder pop. It hurt so bad I started screaming and peed a little. It trickled warm down my leg. Mom came running. Nick let me go.

I ran outside holding my arm. Pain like a lightning bolt shot up my neck and down my fingers. It felt like someone had stabbed me in the shoulder with a poker from the fireplace. I couldn't even turn my head or see or think. The ice cream truck was long gone.

I sat down on the sidewalk and screamed. It was the first time I knew what it was like not to be able to breathe. I couldn't think past this one horrible moment. All I knew was the pain and the panic. A dog started howling. The screen door slammed behind me and

Mom came sprinting out of the house. She gathered me in her arms and loaded me into Thelma's back seat. The doctor in the ER reset my dislocated shoulder, which felt like a thousand pokers jabbed in my arm, but then it went numb and I fell asleep. When we got home, Nick was gone. But the fear had come to stay.

I thought I was going to die out on the sidewalk when I couldn't stop crying or catch my breath. I don't think that anymore. The terror has become familiar. Gina has a lot to say about this particular moment in time. She and Mom and I have talked the subject of Nick into the ground. But they can't talk away the panic. I shake my head to clear the itchy memory.

I wrap myself in a fluffy yellow towel and step into my bedroom. Teresa, my yellow plant, is on the windowsill, soaking up the last of the afternoon light. I named her after Mother Teresa, thinking maybe the saint will hear and work her magic. But the little plant is still not doing great. I lift up her drooping stem with my fingertip. I want to believe that the world is full of miracles, that the good things can outshine the bad. I really do. But if wanting was all it took, I'd have a million friends and no panic attacks. I'd be a real superhero, not just some scared girl in a wig.

The Juarezes' home is not that far from the library. Just two blocks over on Vine Street, where the houses look old, but in that nice respectable way with wraparound porches and short picket fences. These places are nothing like our house, with its peeling white paint and concrete steps that have split away from the foundation so you have to hop over the gap to get to the stoop.

I get hit by a wave of shyness when we stand in front of Homer's dark green door. It was easy to say yes to Homer when we were both covered in dirt by the river. But now I'm here and it feels so much *bigger*. I think this is just regular nerves and not full-on anxiety, but I still count to ten like Gina tells me to do. And then I count to twenty, because ten didn't do a thing. Eventually, Mom breaks the silence.

"Go on, knock. Or you want me to do it?" She nudges the back of my leg with her knee because her hands are full of watermelon pie.

Before either of us can act, the door swings open. Lucy, dressed like Wonder Woman, unhitches a yellow lasso from her shoulder and yells, "Mom, the librarians are here!" and then throws it at us.

Mom laughs and ducks, but I jump back. The idea of a rope around me right now makes my palms sweat.

"Ooh, I like your blue hair," Lucy says, dragging the rope back toward her.

"Thank you," I say, and touch it and hope it doesn't smell like sweat and grass from the plant rescue.

"Come on! This way!" Lucy shouts, much louder than is necessary.

Mom and I follow her down a narrow hallway with old

creaky floors and into a sunny kitchen that leads out onto a wide porch. Beyond that, empty card tables sit waiting for picnickers in the shady half of the yard. And twinkle lights, like the ones in our teen section, hang from the trees.

I see Homer under the trees and trip in my sandals. He looks *different*. I'm so used to seeing him in cargo shorts and T-shirts with his hair falling in his eyes. But tonight he's wearing a light blue collared shirt and his hair is damp and combed. Suddenly I'm glad Mom made me wear a dress.

When he spots me, my stomach flips. It's just regular nerves. Has to be. I gave a wobbly smile, and he leaves the soccer ball he was kicking around with his older sister, Kat, and jogs over.

"Hi," he says.

"Hi," I say back.

Mom steps forward with an easy smile. "You clean up nice."

"Thank you, Ms. Delancey."

I wipe my hands on my dress. It's the color of cool orange sherbet. I don't know what to say after hi. What do people talk about? Why are we all just standing here? My face hurts from smiling, but I don't know what to do with it if I stop. Thankfully, Mom says, "Now show me to your parents so I can thank them for inviting us," and the circle of silence is broken.

We follow Homer across the grass toward a few people standing around a grill. The whiff of smoky meat on the night air makes my stomach growl. It calms me down a little. The body is a weird thing. Sometimes something like being hungry can pull me back into my body so I stop thinking so much. Matter over mind, I guess. The hamburgers and hot dogs are just starting to sizzle.

"Mom, Dad, this is Ms. Delancey and her daughter, June," Homer announces. Everybody's eyes settle on us. I scooch closer to Mom. She waves her pie-filled hands in a hello.

A woman with dark hair and red cropped pants steps forward. "Homer has told us so much about you," she says, smiling at us both. "I'm Cecilia, and this is my husband, Gabriel." She points to the man at the grill, who shouts, "Daniel! Keep an eye on this, will you?" and ambles over to join us. He is an exact clone of Homer. Same curls and smile. His apron reads: WHY YOU ALL UP IN MY GRILL? Same sense of humor.

"Call me Gabe." His eyes settle on the dish in Mom's hands. "Oh, what have we here?"

"Watermelon pie."

Homer's parents' faces light up with surprise as she hands it over.

It's always fun to see people's reaction to watermelon pie. Not many have heard of it, but it is one of Mom's specialties. She makes it with a graham cracker crust and fresh watermelon juice and gelatin and cream. Then she tops it with a fluffy meringue that feels like you're eating a cloud. It is sweet, cool goodness. Summer in a pie.

We all stand there for a moment, beholding the pie. Then Mr. Juarez says, "Well, I can't wait to try this," and digs his finger right along the edge.

"Dad!" Homer groans.

"Gabe!" Mrs. Juarez whisks the pie away.

"Apologies," Mr. Juarez says, not looking one bit sorry.

Mom smiles. She knows the power of the pie.

Daniel, the replacement griller, turns around to see what the commotion is about. Like Homer, Daniel is dressed neatly in a button-down shirt. His blond hair is fixed so perfectly you can still see the lines from the comb. I bet he uses product. I bet if you touched it, it would be crunchy. He has a nice smile, and he is looking at us curiously.

"What's so exciting over here?" he asks.

"Ms. Delancey has made us an excellent dessert," Mr. Juarez chuckles before turning back to the grill.

"Corinne," Mom says, holding out her hand to shake now that it is free. I watch Daniel's eyes go round as he really looks at her. Mom's effect on men is a lot like her watermelon pie. Tonight she is wearing a gauzy green dress, one of her favorite Goodwill finds, and her red wig is tied back with a daisy-covered scarf. She looks like a wood nymph.

"Uh," Daniel says eloquently.

"Daniel is a professor at Columbia State with Mom," Homer fills in.

And when Daniel still does not speak, Homer adds, "He teaches ethics."

A professor? Fancy.

"That sounds lovely," Mom says.

"Yes, well . . . ," he begins.

Mom smiles at him encouragingly.

Poor Daniel. He had just begun to recover the power of speech. But that smile undoes him again.

"Well, uh, yes, well . . ."

Homer smirks at me, and we leave Daniel to it. Maybe by the end of the night, he'll get past "well."

"What exactly *is* ethics?" I ask Homer as he fishes the soccer ball out from under the trees.

"It's the study of right and wrong," he answers, and bounces the ball from knee to knee.

I glance back at Mom and Daniel under the twinkle lights. Looks like he's speaking in full sentences now. And Mom is nodding along. So, a professor . . . whose job is to *literally* tell the difference between good and evil. That's like having a certificate in goodness, right? Sam stopped by the library again this afternoon before we left, to "test the wireless connection," or so he claimed. But the way he was smiling down at Mom and she was grinning up at him, it looked more like he was testing the "Corinne connection." I study Daniel. He looks close to Mom's age. More importantly, he looks nothing like Nick.

I know I said I wanted this summer to be all about our independence, but if I have to choose between a professor with shiny hair or Sam, the Nick look-alike, I pick the professor.

Homer is eyeing me as we walk across the grass toward his old swing set.

"What?" I ask.

He tilts his head toward Mom and Daniel.

"Just watching the wheels turn, that's all," he says, and takes one creaking swing as I take the other. "It's like watching you play chess," he adds, and grins.

And for the first time tonight, I give him a real smile back. I'm not nervous anymore.

11
Dragonfly Wings

DINNER IS DELICIOUS. WE SIT OUT UNDER THOSE twinkle lights, with torches blazing to keep away the mosquitoes, and eat our fill of burgers and hot dogs and potato salad and elote, a spicy corn on the cob sprinkled with cheese, which I had never had before, but Mom had. She sighs so loudly over it that Mr. Juarez promises to send her home with his secret spice blend. And of course everybody cheers when Mrs. Juarez brings out Mom's watermelon pie. Daniel eats two slices.

It's Daniel I'm thinking about when I set both feet on the wishing rug on Monday, the first day of July. It's only eleven, way too early in the morning for teenagers, so I've got the room practically all to myself. I barely slept last night or the two nights before because I was too excited. I went to a dinner! And I did not panic! And I have a plan to keep Mom away from Sam. I'm so happy

I don't even mind that I'm jumpy from lack of sleep, like I have drunk too many Cokes. This is impossible, however, because Gina won't let me have any. She says caffeine and anxiety don't mix. The yellow pill definitely never made me feel as good as this. So I shouldn't feel one bit bad that I am no longer taking it.

I stand with my sneakers right in the middle of the rug. If life were like chess, this would be my first big move. Well, maybe second, after shaving my head. I close my eyes and wish for Daniel to fall in love with Mom. That's the easy part. Everybody falls in love with Mom. Then I wish for the harder thing: for Mom to fall in love back. Well, maybe not love, but fall in "like" enough to keep Sam away.

I picture it. Mom and me in the kitchen making pecan sandies for the bake sale at the middle school. All my new friends have already told their moms to buy them, because everybody knows Corinne Delancey is the best baker in the land. And then Daniel stops by on his way to the college, where he will teach people how to be as nice and good as himself. He kisses Mom on the cheek and tries to sneak a cookie. Mom swats his hand away and smiles at me and I smile back, as relaxed as a cat on a windowsill, because while Daniel is nice to have around, we both know I am the first and only taste-tester.

"Junie!"

I'm so lost in my pretend life I jump when Homer calls

my name. He's standing by the chessboard. I know I get more jittery when I don't sleep. I hope he didn't see me jump. I'm going to have to make more of an effort to settle down tomorrow in therapy or Gina's going to ask me about my meds. And I'm not supposed to lie.

"Were you meditating?" Homer asks when I take a seat across from him. "You looked so Zen."

"No. I was wishing on the wishing rug."

He nods.

This is what I appreciate about Homer: I can say a thing like that and he just nods as if it makes perfect sense.

"What were you wishing for?" he asks, setting up our pieces. He always lets me be the white.

Here is the moment of truth. Do I tell him about my plans for Mom and Daniel? I've always gone it alone before. But that would be playing it safe. And the girl who shaves her head and ditches her meds and says yes to dinner invitations and starts a garden with stolen plants down by the river does not play it safe.

"I was wishing for a way to make Mom and Daniel get together."

"Intriguing," he says, and then adds in his poetry-reciting voice,

"Love is like flying a kite—
It's light as air
But you better hold on tight."

"Another famous poet?"

"Nope, me," he confesses, and goes a little pink around the ears.

I snort. It is impossible not to. But then I add, "I liked it," because if he didn't laugh at my idea for Mom and Daniel, I'm not going to laugh at his poetry. He smiles down at his chess pieces.

"So you're in? You'll help me?" I ask after we settle into our game.

"Oh, I'm in," he answers without looking up. "Just tell me our plan."

I like the sound of "our."

We find Luis lingering outside Conference Room C. According to him, he is "acting casual" until Nix shows up. We drag him down to the river to help us check on our flowers and to stop him from looking so desperate.

He fetches two small cartons of strawberries from his car on the way. They are the most beautiful strawberries I have ever seen—each one huge and deep red all the way around. When we get down to our garden plot and out from under the watchful eyes of the Tandy, he gives each of us one to try. They taste even better than they look.

"Luis," I say, holding up the green nub that's all I have left. "These are amazing."

"Yes. I know. I grew these."

"You *grew* these?" I ask as Homer reaches for another one and Luis bats his hand away.

"Do not sound so surprised and do not eat all my gifts."

"Ohhhhh, I get it. These are for *Nix*." I shouldn't tease him. But Luis is so teasable at the moment in his neatly pressed linen shirt and shiny shoes. He wouldn't even help us get the gardening tools and watering can from his car for fear of getting "mussed."

"These are for Nicole, yes. I remember she liked the strawberry from your mom's little cakes. But she has not tasted a strawberry until she tastes these." He holds up the little green carton and sniffs it like a bouquet of flowers.

I laugh and catch Homer's eye. We have a quick conversation in eyebrow gestures and mouth twitches and then it's decided, the next step in the Plan.

"Listen, Luis, we need your help," I say, getting down on my knees to see if our little patch of black-eyed Susans needs some water.

He brushes his fingers over the delicate leaves. "The garden is looking good. I will bring you some tomato plants. And marigolds, too. They will keep your bugs away."

"Really? Wow. Thanks!" I say. Homer nudges me. I'm getting off track.

"We have someone special we think June's mom would really hit it off with," Homer says. "And we need tips for getting the two of them together, you know, romantically." I expect Luis to say it's none of our business. But I underestimated his level of in-love-ness. His whole face lights up.

"Your mom, she likes this someone special?" Luis asks me.

I nod, even though I have no idea. I tried watching them at dinner, but Mom and I were at a different table from Daniel. At one point he leaned over and made a joke about Mr. Juarez's apron and she laughed. That has to be good, right?

"Well, then," Luis is saying, walking up and down in the shade of the trees as dragonflies dart up from the river's edge. "If this is new, it must have time and space to grow. They need to get to know each other. Establish roots, like these plants, you understand?"

I do not. But Homer nods.

"You're saying they need to spend some quality time together," Homer says. I raise my eyebrows at him, and he shrugs. "My parents are always complaining about not getting enough 'quality time' alone."

"Sí. They need to learn each other. Jazz or the opera? Salty or sweet? Bridge or poker?" It is so clear that he's talking about Nix now, we release him from garden duty.

He promises to bring more plants and love tips tomorrow and then carefully makes his way up the hill in his shiny shoes, ready to resume his post by her door.

"He's right, you know," Homer adds when we're alone again. "It's going to take more than one dinner at my house to make it stick."

"But how are we going to get them together again?" I begin to water our plants once more for good measure. They really are doing well. They look sturdier than before. I'm feeling shaky, though. It must be the heat. When I stand up from crouching, my vision goes black for a second and I have to put my hands on my knees so I don't fall over.

When the blackness fades, I glance over at Homer. He's clearing a few clumps of grass from in between the rows. Because he's not looking at me, what I do next is easier. I reach up and pull off my wig. It's immediately twenty degrees cooler. But when I catch him looking, I start to tug it back on.

"There she is."

I pause. "Who?"

"Rebel June," he says, standing.

I keep the wig off, cradling it in my hand like a pet.

"What, blue hair isn't enough?" I ask.

"Nah, it's not that." He brushes the dirt off his hands. "I just think this suits you."

"Well, uh . . ." Oh good. I sound like Daniel.

Homer doesn't notice. He talks right over me. "So, listen. The library's closed on Thursday, for the Fourth of July, right?"

"Yeah."

"Perfect. We can plan to 'accidentally' meet at the parade downtown," he says, using air quotes around "accidentally."

I feel every tiny new hair on my head prickle. And I make myself keep very, very still. He's talking about the big Independence Day parade down at the square. The one with the floats and the band and the food stands and the bouncy houses and ponies and hot, crowded sidewalks with all the side streets blocked off so a person can't even escape if they wanted to. It's an anxious person's worst nightmare. But he's also right. It's the perfect place for two potential lovebirds to *accidentally* meet.

Overhead the sky is a vast, limitless stretch of blue. I run my fingers through the blue hair in my hand. I can feel the panic buzzing just under the surface of my skin, like the sound of so many dragonfly wings.

"Sure. Sounds good."

Independence Day

GINA HANDS ME A SERIES OF PAINT SWATCHES. I am supposed to choose the color that fits my mood. I find a deep reddish orange one called Ginger and hand it to her, hiding my torn and bitten fingernails as best I can.

I tell her the color reminds me of Thelma, and Thelma makes me feel safe. I do *not* tell her that everything about the Fourth of July parade makes me feel the opposite.

I reach down to pat Rochester. He's standing in as a "therapy dog" today, meaning Gina's pet sitter is out of town and she can't run home to let him out between appointments. He sighs and rolls over on my foot.

"Have you been working on your breathing techniques?"

I nod, eyes on Rochester.

"And the new medication," she continues. "The lethargy has lessened?"

Fortunately, she's making a note on her yellow legal pad and not looking at me.

"Oh yeah. Definitely less." Which is the truth. No lethargy here. I am as keyed up as a piano.

She stops writing. Studies me. Clicks her pen. Uh-oh.

"But you're still sleeping through the night?"

I pat Rochester. I can feel him shiver under my palm. Gina narrows her eyes.

"I planted a garden," I say.

This makes her blink.

"Well." She tucks a stray hair back behind her ear. "I think that's lovely. I told you it might be good for you."

"Yeah. I found this gardening book on the returns shelf and my friend Homer is helping. And Luis, the one I told you about who gave me the seeds, is teaching us how to take care of it."

Gina leans forward so our knees almost touch. She seems delighted by this wealth of information.

"Sounds like you're making some good friends *and* some good progress this summer," she says, writing fast and furiously on her notepad while Rochester farts contentedly at my feet.

By the time I'm done telling her about the plant rescue mission and the dinner at Homer's, our session is over. There's no time left to quiz me again about the little yellow pills.

That night I tell Mom I want to go to the parade. Therapy plus gardening plus an hour spent with Homer googling Daniel on the library computers finally convinced me to go through with it. According to his faculty page on the Columbia State website, Daniel volunteers at the food bank and has season tickets to the symphony. He has "safe bet" written all over him—and a safe bet is exactly what I need so Mom and I can keep being our fierce selves without too much intervention.

"You want to *what*?"

Mom turns to me from where she's julienning carrots for the salad. Her face could not be more surprised if I had said I wanted to set sail for the sun.

"I want to go to the parade down on the square for the Fourth."

"There'll be lots of people," she says.

"I know."

"And loud music."

"I know."

"And it will be hot."

I thump our plates down on the table harder than is necessary.

"Mom, I *know*."

She eyes me suspiciously and begins to open her mouth when the screen door creaks open and we hear a knock on the front door.

"You expecting someone?" I ask. But she's already

wiping her hands on a red dish towel and heading down the hall. She glances at herself in the hallway mirror, pauses to smooth her hair. I don't like that one bit.

"Well, hello," she says in the voice she uses for company. "Thanks for dropping by."

"It's no problem," a deep male voice says, and I march up to the door.

There he is, Sam, in jeans and a blue T-shirt that matches his baby-blue eyes, which remind me so much of Nick that I wince.

"What are *you* doing here?" I say.

Mom tsks at me. "June, manners!"

Seems highly *un*mannered to drop by at dinnertime, but nobody asks me.

"Hi, June." Sam ducks under the doorway, looking much too tall for our tiny house. "I'm just returning your mom's laptop. She asked me to take a look at it to see if I could find out why it was running so slowly."

I watch him slip her silver work laptop out of his geeky satchel and hand it to her. She *blushes*. I cross my arms. The hallway is narrow and I am the third in line, but I squeeze in next to Mom.

"You couldn't give this to her at her place of business?"

"June!"

"You're right, that would have been smarter, June," he says, and smiles down at me. "But I'm off for the rest of the week and I figured she might want it over the holiday."

"Thank you so much," Mom says, touching her hair again. "And you were correct. Would you excuse me for one minute?" She puts a calming hand on my shoulder and then goes down the hallway, past me, and into the kitchen.

I am alone with Sam.

He blinks at me and keeps smiling, tall and nervous and hunched, like a baby giraffe, which is very un-Nick. But I still want him gone. When he clears his throat and a long pause follows, I do not fill it.

Mom isn't gone long. I watch as she hands him a tin, my *favorite* tin with the green and white stripes.

"Lemon squares for your trouble," she explains.

He thanks her. He backs out the door. She stands in the glow of the streetlight to wave goodbye.

The entire interaction takes less than five minutes. It all seems innocent enough. But I'm no fool.

At dinner I say, "So, we're on for the Fourth." It's not a question.

She studies me over the pork chops.

"Okay. If that's what you want," she says after an eternity.

"That's what I want."

It's been so many days since I've slept more than a few hours in a row that when I blink awake on Thursday morning, the edges of my vision are blurry. I turn over under the thin sheet and feel the damp patches where I sweated through my T-shirt. This also happens when I'm anxious. I sweat in the night like my body cannot possibly hold that much worry and water at the same time.

I can't think about that now. The sun is shining and it's going to be another cloudless day. Cloudless and hot. Ninety-eight degrees, but it's supposed to feel like one hundred and five. I checked the weather on Mom's laptop at two and three and five in the morning. I'll never admit this to Mom, but I have to give Sam credit. Her computer runs lightning fast now. I get up slowly so the dizziness that comes with sleeplessness doesn't make me fall over. Maybe I can take a nap before everything starts. We're supposed to meet Homer and his family and—oh, what a surprise!—Daniel, by the flagpole at noon.

I tuck my finger into the soil under Teresa's drooping stem like Luis showed me. It's plenty wet, but she's still not doing well. I move her to my dresser. Maybe she needs a break from the sun and to rest some more, like me. I crawl back into bed and pull the covers over my head.

At 11:46, Mom and I hop into the car, ready to go. The nap was a bust, but after two bowls of Lucky Charms and sneaking one of Mom's leftover lemon squares, I am more awake. My blue tank top is the exact same shade as my hair, and my new red sequined sunglasses glitter in the sunlight. I made Mom change three times. If this is going to be love at second sight, it has to be perfect. We settled on a red-and-white-checkered sleeveless dress that she found at a thrift store back in New Orleans. With her red platform sandals and red hair swept up in a high ponytail, she looks like a movie star.

"Mom, get moving! We are meeting the Juarezes in less than fifteen minutes!"

She gives me a look over her cat-eye sunglasses and takes her time buckling her seat belt and adjusting the mirror. No one hurries Mom. I am sitting on my hands to keep from banging them on the dashboard. *Finally* she turns the key and Thelma coughs and whines before . . . shuddering into silence. I take a deep breath as Mom turns the key again. This happens sometimes. Occasionally, Thelma just needs a warm-up. But this time it's like she's not even trying—just whining like a coffee grinder. Mom sighs, gets out, and pops the hood.

I crank my window down and lean out to watch her. I don't trust myself to leave the vehicle. I focus on *not* rocking back and forth. This is it. This is how all my plans get ruined. I hunch down in my seat again when Mom disappears inside the house to search for Thelma-fixing tools.

Any minute now, Homer and his family and Daniel will arrive at the flagpole and time will pass. Eventually, they will wander off to buy some barbecue from the food trucks lining the square and Daniel will come with them. He'll meet a woman. She'll be selling pottery at one of those arts-and-crafts booths and he will ask about the handmade vase, even though he doesn't need a vase. But he likes the way she smiles at him and the clay under her nails. He will tell her he is a professor and she will run a hand through her hair. Then he will buy her vase and fill it with flowers from the florist down the street and he will bring it back to her. They'll make a date to talk about pottery and ethics. And Mom and I will still be here, in our gravel driveway, stuck to these hot leather seats like eggs in a pan.

The clock on the car ticks over to 11:54. Mom comes back and holds a blue jug up to my open window.

"Just needs some coolant," she says, but then pauses. I must look bad—weird and wired and *not* okay. I slide my sunglasses back down over my eyes.

"Great," I say, keeping my voice steady and rolling up the window. The heat swallows me whole. Mom walks to the front, pours in the coolant, and lets the hood slam shut without another word.

We lose seven minutes circling downtown, turning the wrong way down one-way roads and reversing into church parking lots only to be told they're off-limits for "the event." I pick, pick, pick at the peeling leather on the side of my seat where Mom cannot see. When we come to a dead stop in front of a row of orange cones behind the Bank of America, I rub my eye sockets hard with my fists, hoping Mom will think I'm tired instead of close to tears.

She puts the brake on and sets a hand on my shoulder blade, light as a bird landing.

"Let's splurge, huh?"

I lift my head. She's pointing at a paid lot where a lady in a green lawn chair is holding up a sign and waving people through.

"It's ten dollars," I say, but I am already leaning forward, willing Thelma toward that ocean of empty spaces.

"Worth it," Mom says, reversing us away from the cones and to freedom.

Mom complains about running in heels, but she does it anyway because I am ten steps ahead and not slowing. We get to the flagpole by 12:23. A high school dance team does some warm-up kicks on the stage in front of the courthouse. There are plenty of people here, waving tiny flags and pushing strollers and eating shaved ice. None of them is Homer.

I make a loop, all the way around the grassy area where the flag is hanging like a wet rag in this windless heat. They are not here! We just spent half a gallon of coolant and ten dollars and they've already gone. I sit down on the curb where Mom can't see me.

My head itches and I want to rip my wig off, but there's a group of teenagers a few feet away, scrolling on their phones, and I don't want them to notice. I pick all the sequins off my sunglasses instead. The glue holding them on is soft from the heat and they come off slimy and sticky in my hands. Stupid, cheap glasses. I throw them into the street, where a shadow falls over them. It's Homer. He holds out a funnel cake toward me, dropping bits of powdered sugar on my knees.

"Sorry we're late," he says, sitting down next to me on the curb and reaching over to pick up my de-sequined sunglasses. "Lucy had to stop to get this." He tears off a warm doughy corner and holds it out to me. I wipe my nose on my sleeve and take it.

"You okay?"

I chew slowly, letting the buttery dough dissolve on my tongue. I pay attention to the sensation—try to pull myself out of my head and back into the moment. It also buys me some time.

"Yeah. I'm okay. We just got here too. Car trouble." My voice sounds mostly normal. You'd never know I was screaming in my head ten seconds ago.

"Bummer."

"Yeah."

"Is Daniel with you?" I ask, trying to get myself back on track.

"He's with my mom." He jerks his thumb over his

shoulder. "They stopped by the used bookstore."

Mom's probably beyond worried now that I've been gone so long. I scan the crowd for her, but there's barely a gap in the bodies. It's just elbows and knees and fanny packs. My heart thumps loud in my ears. We had a plan. But now I can't make myself move from this tiny circle of space. Homer stands and holds out a hand to pull me up. I make myself take it.

We find Mom and Mr. Juarez at one of the demonstration booths. Someone is showing them how a new, all-organic stain remover can get red wine out of white carpet.

"And it's safe enough to drink! But I wouldn't." The demonstrator's Adam's apple bobs up and down like a cork when he laughs. He looks too young to be selling anything.

"Mom," I interrupt. "I'm hot. Want to go check out Book Man Book Woman?"

"*There* you are! We sent Homer to find you." She squeezes my shoulder and then looks past me toward the bookstore. "Let's do it, baby. I need some air-conditioning."

Book Man Book Woman is our favorite used bookstore because it's run by an older couple, Mrs. Martha and Mr. Paul, who have no organizational system whatsoever. Spy novels are piled next to devotionals. New releases are way in the back, but also sometimes by the checkout counter. It's like a whole store of recent returns. Whenever the library has leftover books from their quarterly sale, we drive them over here.

Mom takes my hand, which I know is clammy, but she doesn't notice. Homer and Mr. Juarez follow. Between all the sweating bodies and panting dogs and kids blowing bubbles and spilling their lemonade in the street, I am more than ready to hide inside the cool of the bookstore.

The bell over the door jingles when we walk in, and the familiar smell of paper and musty carpet greets me like a hug. It's more calming than a thousand deep breaths and counts to ten. Mr. Paul is running a booth out front to try to draw parade-goers inside, but Mrs. Martha is in her usual spot, perched on a stool by the register.

"My girls!" she calls. Her arm wobbles when she waves.

Mom makes like she wants to go over and chat, but Homer nudges me and points to Daniel's blond head over in the corner, where graphic novels are jumbled with the cookbooks. For the first time, I feel like our plan is back on track. I wish it made my insides settle down a little more. I tug her toward him.

"Well, what a surprise!" I say when Daniel turns at the sound of our approach. Mom smiles, but gives me the side-eye. She knows something's up. I keep smiling until it hurts, beaming *be friendly* vibes at her like she always does to me. Daniel is wearing a cherry-red polo shirt and shorts with little blue pinstripes. He matches Mom perfectly.

"Well, hello, ladies." He holds out his hand to Mom. I can tell she wants to pull me outside and quiz me about this "surprise," but politeness wins. She hesitates a second and then shakes his hand.

Once contact has been made, Homer and I get out as fast as we can, winding our way through the narrow aisles to the front of the store, where Mrs. Juarez is purchasing a giant stack of hardbacks. They must be expensive, because Mrs. Martha hums to herself as she rings them up.

"Where's Homer?" Mrs. Juarez asks.

"What do you mean? He was just behind me." I turn around, but the aisle is deserted. I start backtracking. He better not be hovering around Mom and Daniel. He heard what Luis said. They need some alone time.

But Homer is not hovering. Homer is reading. I find him crouched down in the poetry section. Big surprise. He's cradling a copy of Shel Silverstein's *A Light in the Attic.*

When I kick his shoe to get his attention, he holds the book up in awe. "This is a signed copy," he whispers, and shows me an illegible scribble on the title page.

"You don't have to whisper. We're not in the library,"

I say, louder than necessary. But he's already back to his book. He has forgotten all about me. It shouldn't bother me that he's having such a good time today. But it does. He has no idea how hard this is for me.

I kick him again when Mom starts calling for us from the front.

"Just buy it if you want it so bad," I say.

"I know, but . . ."

"But what?" I huff.

"But it's expensive, and I already promised Lucy I'd buy her one of those unicorn kites they're selling in front of the toy store. That'll be the last of my allowance."

I don't say anything. But I think as loud as I can, *Must be nice to get an allowance!*

In the end, he takes the book up to Mrs. Martha and puts it on hold. I think he's hoping Lucy will forget about the kite in all the commotion now that the parade is starting.

When we spill out onto the sidewalk, I spy Mom and Daniel standing next to each other. But they're not talking. Why aren't they talking?

I watch Daniel watching Mom. He seems about to say something, but he can't get it out. Dark rings of sweat have spread under the arms of his red polo. He keeps lifting his arms to check. *Yes, Daniel, they're still there.* Mom leans around him and shades her eyes to look down the street at the high school marching band coming around the corner in their maroon-and-gold tasseled uniforms. The brash clanging of cymbals makes my ears hurt. *Everything* about this day hurts.

I shove my way to her and yell in her ear, "What are you doing?!"

"What do you mean?" she shouts back. She starts to turn to me, to bend down, to really pay attention, but I look away so she can't read my face.

"Oh, look. Trombones!" I yell, because that is what normal people do. I can't let her see how hard this is for me. If she's worried about me, she'll never pay attention to Daniel.

There's a pressure right behind my eyes that feels like a wasp is trying to burrow into my brain. Someone's elbow is digging into my shoulder blade. A little girl in a *PAW Patrol* mask knocks into me and her Go-Gurt drips onto my leg. It's Lucy. She gives me a wave. Homer is behind her, not even watching the parade. He's looking back at his book sitting on Mrs. Martha's desk.

By the time the baton twirlers round the corner by the big stage, I am wrung out—shaky and weak. I need to eat or lean against something. I should have tried to sleep more this morning. But wait! Something is *actually* happening with Daniel and Mom. He's leaning over and speaking. And she's grinning. Grinning! Finally. She starts to reply, but Homer steps forward, between them.

I yank his shirtsleeve. "Get back here," I say. But he's looking at the road.

"Look!" he shouts, and points.

Now that the band has passed, the floats are starting to come around the corner. The first one is decorated like a giant cake covered in glitter and looped with lace to look like icing. And Nix is standing right on the very top. *Nix.* She's wearing a long red robe and a *crown.* Behind her a man kneels to stretch out her robe so everyone can read the writing on the back: *Little Crowne Bakery.* The man looks up right as the float passes us. It's Luis! What is *happening*?

Mom whistles through her fingers and they both turn toward us. Luis grins. Nix winks. I keep blinking to see if I'm hallucinating.

After they turn the corner and disappear, Mom turns to Mrs. Juarez, who's trying to wipe down Lucy with a wad of napkins because she's dripping with Go-Gurt, and asks, "Does Nix own the Little Crowne Bakery?"

"Who? Oh, you mean Nicole. Nicole *Crowne*," she says. "She does."

Mom's mouth falls open. Daniel sees her and laughs. It comes out as a giggle. That's unfortunate. But Mom's not paying him any attention. She's staring after that float.

"Mom?" I tug on her dress. *"Mom,"* I whine, hating the sound of it. "Can we go see the Irish step dancers?"

I don't care one bit about the Irish step dancers, but they're walking onto the stage across the square and there are chairs set up in front. I'm hoping to get Daniel and Mom away from this mass of people so they can talk more. And also, I need to sit down.

"Oh, uh, sure. If that's what you want, Junebug." She sounds distracted, but she smiles and puts a hand on my cheek. It's cool despite the heat. All of a sudden, I want to be home with her. We could lie on our worn-out red couch in the living room and prop open the front and back screen doors to let in the breeze.

But sometimes the bigger goal is worth the smaller sacrifice. That's what Gina tells me when she wants me to try giving up sugary drinks or screen time after six p.m. "We're aiming for quality of life here, June," she says, "and it's the little things that make all the difference." Irish step is a small price to pay for Mom's happiness.

So I lead Mom and Daniel and the Juarezes through the crowd toward the stage. We find seats in the last available row of chairs, which happens to be in the very front, next to the speakers, directly in the sun. At least I get to sit.

Homer is next to me and he elbows me when Mom and Daniel start to talk. Mom asks him all about his classes. Where he went to college. How he ended up in Tennessee. And Daniel is answering in complete, if formal, sentences. I wish he would loosen up a little. Also, he should reapply sunscreen. His forehead looks as bright as a tomato. But they *are* talking, at least.

"Love's labor's won, I think," Homer whispers, and I am sure it's a line from a poem and I forget to be annoyed with him for a second, because even though this day has *not* gone according to plan and the backs of my legs have melted to this plastic seat, I think he might be right.

Up on the stage, the dancers get into position and freeze, like they're waiting for a nonexistent curtain to be pulled up. I study their hair, which is twisted into complicated ribbons and braids, and wonder if I could do that with my wig or if it would mess it up. Soon they start shooting each other glances without moving their faces. I recognize that look. Panic. Something's not right. They are still frozen in place. Seconds pass. Their smiles start to slip. I am nervous *for* them.

Because we're so close to the stage, I can see behind the backdrop. People scurry around the courthouse, checking power cords and speaking into headphones. One guy dressed all in black darts out from behind the stage with a satchel slung over his shoulder. I recognize that satchel, and his impossible tallness when he kneels in front of the speaker and pulls out a laptop. *No.*

"Sam!" Mom exclaims.

When he turns, his eyes settle on Mom and positively *sparkle.* I'm not the only one who notices. Next to her, Daniel is suddenly very busy with a flyer for a free tune-up at Roy's Auto Repair. I drop my head against the seat.

"What are you doing here?" Mom and Sam ask at the same time. And then they *laugh* at the exact same time. Sam has a laugh as deep and rumbling as thunder.

"June and I came to watch the parade," Mom says, turning a brilliant smile on me, which I do not return. I am counting my breaths.

"That reminds me," Sam says to me, like he has all the time in the world and there are not dancers onstage beginning to look seasick. "Your mom told me you've taken in a sick plant," he says, and I wonder when Mom had the time to share this information. "I have an app for you if you're interested. It plays music that encourages growth. You play it for the plants," he adds.

"Awesome," I say when Mom elbows me in the ribs.

Sam doesn't notice. He's touching the earpiece on his headset and tilting his head like a secret service agent. Then he turns back to us. "Sorry, I've got to get back to work. I'm volunteering with the tech department today, and we seem to be having some trouble with our sound system."

As if on cue, the speakers screech. It's the sound of an animal in a trap, of knives across a plate, of the bus brakes at your stop on the first day back to school. It is the worst sound in the world. And it jerks something loose in me. I grab my ears. It's too much. Thelma not starting and sweaty bodies everywhere and a too-loud band and Go-Gurt sticky on my leg and Sam breaking

up Mom and Daniel before they can properly con-
nect and Homer relaxed and happy through it all. My
stomach cramps. I have to get out of here.

When I stand, everything goes black. I fall forward
and one knee slams into the hot asphalt. Mom gasps
and touches my back. Homer shouts something over
the screeching speakers. His hand lands on mine and
I flinch.

Somehow I manage to get up again and limp a few
steps. And then I *run*. I run past the lemonade stand
and the shaved ice and the demonstrators and I cut
across the grass under the limp flag.

I take the corner at the bookstore too quickly and
smack into someone so hard I bite my tongue and taste
blood.

"Oh my God. Are you kidding me?" the person gasps.

No. It *can't* be.

"Walk much?" Allyson asks. Jasmine stands next to
her. They're wearing matching blue-and-white tie-dyed
sundresses. They haven't seen me since school let out. I
saw *them* in the bathroom, but they don't know that. I
hold my breath.

"June? Is that you?" Jasmine asks, staring at my
electric blue hair. Allyson narrows her eyes at me. *I am
a lion. I am a lion. I am a lion.*

But then Allyson smiles and says, "Cool look," and
it's a tiny miracle in a terrible day. I *am* a lion.

I open my mouth to say thank you, but before I can, she turns to Jasmine and asks, "You know who she looks like? *Violet, you're turning violet, Violet!* Get it, Jas?"

She points from my hair to my blue shirt that I was so proud of this morning.

"I love Willy Wonka. Don't you?" she says to me.

I swallow and swallow the sour taste of blood. I need to throw up.

Behind me the speakers screech again, and Allyson and Jasmine look past me. I don't wait for another chance. I break into a run and do not stop. I pump my arms and legs until they don't even feel like they're part of my body. Until my feet are blistered and my shirt is slicked to me with sweat. Until my brain grows fuzzy and the world tips sideways. When my head clears from the panicky fog, I am on a shady tree-lined street, alone.

13

The Wilderness

IT HAPPENS THIS WAY SOMETIMES. NOT QUICK LIKE a panic attack, but slow, like a sunburn. It'll come creeping in over hours or days or weeks and then *bam!* I'm knocked sideways by the pain and left blistered and raw from my own emotions. Time is tricky too. In the space between losing myself and coming back again, there is always a gap.

Mom finds me, minutes or hours later, curled up on my side with my back to some stranger's fence. A bluebird chirps on the branch above me.

My wig is gone. Lost somewhere in flight. Mom gathers me in her arms to help me up. Somehow we make it back to the car. Thelma starts on the first try.

And then we are home and through the screen door without so much as a hiccup. This is how it goes. When you have nothing left to lose, the world turns in your favor.

I lie under my sheets and watch the ceiling fan twirl. Mom helped me take a bath like she used to when I was little, filling the tub with bubbles that smell like strawberries. Then she helped me dress in a clean white T-shirt and pajama shorts. She comes in now with a cool rag for my forehead and a glass of water tinkling with ice. The neighbor kids are waving sparklers in the street. I hear their laughter and catch the whiff of smoke through the open window. The sun is on its way down.

Mom sits on the edge of my bed and lays a hand on my foot that's tucked under the covers. I haven't spoken since she found me. I can tell it worries her. But those are *her* worries. I can't take on any more. She took off her wig, and I wonder if it's because she doesn't want me to feel bad that I lost mine. Who cares? What's one more thing to feel bad about?

After a while, she gets up and tugs the sheets all the way up to my chin, exactly how I like them. She might be crying. I can't tell. Before she leaves, she whispers, "Get some rest, Junebug."

Rest. If only.

But the thing is, I do sleep. I sleep like the dead. I sleep like I have never slept before. I wake once to the pop and sizzle of fireworks somewhere far away. And then I'm asleep again and next thing I know the sun is stretching its bright wings across my floor. By the angle of the light, it's late, afternoon maybe. I don't know if it is the following day or the next. I guess it doesn't matter. If I never leave the house again, they can all be tomorrows.

Mom hears me moving and pads barefoot into my room. She's holding a steaming plate of her croissant French toast, and even though I smell the syrup and the butter, I can't make myself sit up and take it from her. She's hard to look at. How many times can one person disappoint another? I am the reason she isn't fixing her French toast at an outdoor café down on Market Street in New Orleans. I am the reason we live in this tiny house with the broken steps and chain-link fence. *I am the reason she is not a strong, independent female.* She could go anywhere and be anything if she didn't have me.

I turn away from her, roll over, and go back to sleep. Time passes.

It's nighttime again and my body's aching to stand, so I slide out of bed, careful to skip the creaky board by the window so Mom doesn't hear. I see her through the open door, asleep in a chair in the hallway so she can be near me. I move to the dresser, where Teresa sits. She looks the same. I don't know what I thought I'd find. Maybe I thought she'd be all shriveled and dried, a twig of her former self. But she's still here, still yellow around the edges, but hanging on. She's so much smaller than her seedling sisters, which are growing taller and greener every day in their home by the river.

I move her back over to the windowsill so she can catch some moonlight, and that's when I see it, my blue wig, brushed and resting on the knob at the end of my bed. Mom must have gone back for it, or maybe Homer found it, if he cared enough to go looking. It hurts to think about Homer. Maybe he's forgotten about me already. I would if I could. And just like that, I am tired again. I crawl back into bed and turn over, search for a cool spot in the sheets, and wait for sleep to take me again.

There's something wet scraping against my hand. I jerk awake. It's Rochester. Rochester, the greyhound, is licking my hand with his warm, rough tongue and staring at me with woeful eyes. I cup my fingers around his snout and touch my nose to his. We breathe each other in.

Apparently, Gina makes house calls.

From the doorway, she says, "I think he might be a little in love with you."

"That makes two of us," I say. My voice comes out scratchy and low. I swallow a couple of times and sit up, which is all the invitation Rochester needs to launch his deer-sized body onto my bed.

"How're you doing, kiddo?" Gina asks, leaning

against the doorframe in jeans and a white flowy tank top. I've never seen her with her hair down. She looks almost as young as Mom.

"I'm all right," I say. The lie is so obvious we glide right past it.

"If your life had a soundtrack, what song would be playing right now?"

"Anything by Sam Smith."

"I see." If Gina had a pen, she would click it.

If I could write a song, I would name it "Melancholy" and it would be this—the sound of two people, in the quiet, waiting for something to give. I lean back against the headboard. Gina crosses her arms. Mom is suspiciously absent. I can hear her puttering around in the kitchen, clinking cutlery and dishes like she's trying to stay out of the way and also hear everything at the same time.

"You haven't been taking your medication, have you?" Gina asks.

She already knows the answer.

"When is the last time you slept more than a few hours in a row?"

I open my mouth, but Gina holds up her hand to add, "*Not* counting the last few days."

I shake my head, rubbing Rochester's velvety ear like the worry stone Gina once gave me, which I never used.

"What about your breathing techniques or your safe

people? Have you told your mother what's going on?"

She always says "safe *people*," as if I have anyone other than Mom. I never even told Homer about the anxiety. I am still superhero June to him. Or I was.

I stay quiet. What is there to say? Eventually, Gina sighs and moves into the room to sit on the end of my bed, tucking her legs up underneath her just like she does in her white chair during our sessions. Rochester groans, like sharing his space is almost too much to bear.

"If you think about it," she says, "worry is fairly creative. It is!" she adds when I raise my eyebrows. "It's an act of the imagination. And you have an *excellent* imagination. But none of us can know what's to come or how to control it when it does. All we can do is learn how to live in the moment as best we can."

She places a hand on Rochester's back, but it's as if she's placing her hand on me. The clinking of her bracelets is soothing.

"I'm here to help you. You don't have to tackle it all on your own. But you *do* need to be honest with me and your mother. If the medication is making you feel funny, tell us. We can try something else. It's all about trial and error."

I've had so many errors. When is it going to be all right?

Gina keeps talking. "And it doesn't have to be forever.

I want to help you find an even keel. It's like a sailboat that needs righting after a storm. This is all meant to give you the lift you need, so you can power under your own steam."

She shakes her head. "I'm mixing my metaphors here. Sorry." I don't know what she's even talking about. I focus on Rochester's side, moving up and down under my hand in a steady rhythm.

"Remember what I told you at the beginning of summer? None of this is a quick fix. You practice. You trust me. You trust the process. And together we find a way through, okay?"

The banging around in the kitchen has stopped and Mom appears in the doorway, holding a dish towel. She comes in and places her fingers against my cheek. Between Mom and Gina and Rochester, there are more bodies in this room than ever before.

After Gina leaves, dragging a whining Rochester with her, and Mom watches me eat a bowl of vegetable soup, I move Teresa to my bedside table and crawl back under the sheets. I'm sure Gina's speech was nice. But I'm tired of "the process." I just want to rest.

Luis stands in my doorway, holding his hat in one hand and a small potted plant in the other. The sun is setting again.

"Honey, you have a visitor," Mom says from behind him, which seems obvious and probably what she should have started with before letting Luis into my room.

I sit up slowly, conscious of my bare head. Mom flicks the light on and I squint. Outside the sky is fading into purple. It's that lonesome hour between daytime and dark, when the world doesn't know who it wants to be.

"Hola, June. We have missed you at the library," he says, and shuffles into my room.

What day is it? I wonder.

"It's Saturday, baby," Mom says, reading my mind as she sets two of our pink plastic glasses, filled with iced tea, on my bedside table.

Two days. I have been in my white room under my white sheets for almost two whole days. Maybe this is how I survive. I stay in my room and let the sun keep looping around me. I could do it—with enough library books and a decent chess set.

Mom pulls one of our kitchen chairs into the room for Luis.

He sits next to me. "Nicole sends her love."

I remember the float, Nix looking regal with Luis by her side. Did she need a pair of hands and Luis was there? Or is it more than that? I think of sweet Luis and how kind he is to people and plants and catch myself hoping so. Then I shake my head. She just keeps him around because it's convenient. Gina says worry is an act of the imagination. Hope is too. But hope hurts worse because it never comes true.

Luis looks around the room. Anywhere but at me. He doesn't know what to say, now that he's here. He glances down at his hands and seems surprised to find a flowerpot there. He places it next to our glasses of tea. It is tall, with spindly stems that are covered in dark purple buds.

"Lavender," he says, and pinches off a few of the buds. He rubs them together in his palms and then cups his hands and holds them out to me.

"Please, smell."

I don't have to lean forward to catch the scent. It's minty and spicy all at once.

"It is soothing, you see?"

I close my eyes. He brought a plant because he thought it would soothe me. His kindness hurts. After a few seconds, I hear the scrape of his chair across the floor as he stands to leave. When he whispers goodbye, I pretend to sleep because I don't trust myself not to cry.

Once he's gone, I pick another lavender bud and lift it to my nose. It reminds me of something.

The summer I am six, Nick is gone most of the time, opening for another (and better) country music singer. One lazy afternoon after her work at the music store, Mom decides to get out Nana and Poppy's old hand-crank ice cream maker.

She stirs cream and milk and loads of bright purple buds just like these in a pot on the stove. Our house fills with the same sweet and spicy smell. She lets me beat in the egg yolks and sugar. *Slower!* She laughs and holds my hand on the wooden spoon.

We let it cool and then carry it out to the backyard, where the barrel sits with the ice and salt already packed in tight. Mom helps me pour it inside the metal canister and cover the lid with towels. I crank the big handle until it gets too hard for my six-year-old arms. Then she takes over while I hold the lid steady. I'm sweating, little gnats from the uncut grass sticking to me. But my hands are freezing. I'm hotcold. It's weird and exciting.

It takes all afternoon, and when we're done, Mom doesn't bother with bowls. She passes me my favorite spoon with the ladybugs on the handle and we shimmy the lid off right there in the yard and take turns dipping into the lavender ice cream. It is the softest, sweetest, *strangest* thing I ever tasted. I can still taste it.

I bury my head in the sheets, wishing I was six again.

On Sunday, I start to hate my bed. Mom says never to use that word, but honestly, I can't even look at my rumpled sheets and pillow with the dried drool on it without wanting to throw it all out the window. I shower until the hot water runs out and pull on shorts and a tank top and carry Teresa with me into the living room, where Mom is standing *on* the coffee table in her cutoff jean shorts and ratty Mardi Gras T-shirt.

"What are you doing?" My voice is raspy from lack of use.

She points to a row of paint cans by the front door.

"I'm tired of all this white. Our house needs some *personality*. Hand me those."

I pass her a pile of old sheets and do not mention that Keith was the one who picked white. Speaking of no personality.

She climbs down and together we shake the sheets over our old red couch and flea-market rug. We move the lamp with the pink silk tassels into the corner.

"I'm thinking baby blue for this ceiling and coral for the kitchen."

I nod. I see what's going on. She's giving us a fresh start. This is how Mom and I speak best. Through doing. I don't have the heart to tell her a coat of paint isn't going to make it all better. I may be up and showered, but the panic and sadness still trail me like shadows.

We prop open the front and back screen doors to get a breeze going and borrow stepladders from our neighbors. And then we get to work.

The scabs on my knee from falling at the parade pull as I climb up onto the kitchen counter. I can't think about the parade. I focus on the paint—the sharp smell and the wet gloopy sound it makes when I open the lid. I'm painting a narrow strip of peachy orange above the window when a flash of color in the backyard catches my eye. I set my paintbrush on the edge of the sink and carefully climb down. I can't remember the last time I went into our yard.

"Mom, I'm getting some air," I call back toward the living room, where she's dripping more blue paint on her arms than she's getting on the ceiling.

"All right, baby," she yells.

I tiptoe down the hall, careful not to brush against the wet walls. Mom got a little carried away and painted the whole hall coral. It's like walking into the sunset.

I step out the door and into another world.

Our patchy lawn is now a field of pink and orange and red and yellow and white. There are sunflowers and daisies and poppies in a million colors. By the fence line, I see tiny little violets like the ones painted on my old tea party set. It's like stepping into a painting. Only the painting is moving in the breeze.

I sit down on the back step. It's so beautiful, it almost hurts to look at. How did this happen? The last time I sat here was in the deep darkness of night on the first day of summer, and the lawn was more dirt than anything else. I shake my head and spot a cluster of black-eyed Susans under the kitchen window.

Luis! He gave me that packet of wildflower seeds the first day I met him. But these *can't* be those flowers. I threw the seeds away. I dumped them right in the trash can and slammed down the lid. I didn't check their planting zone like my *ABCs of Gardening* book says. I didn't turn over the soil like Luis showed me. I didn't even let them hit the soil! But here they are. A bumblebee zooms past me and dives headfirst into the flowery wilderness.

For the first time since the parade, I stop thinking. There's no way to explain this. It's an *actual* miracle.

I sprint inside.

"Mom, you have to see this!" I drag her down from the coffee table to show her.

"June, what in the world?"

When she steps outside, her mouth falls open. Then she laughs and it makes *me* laugh, a real one. I run inside and grab a jam jar from the cabinet. As we're filling it with daisies and poppies and sunflowers, I tell her, "I want to paint my room."

"Yeah?"

I nod. She grins.

"What'd you have in mind?"

I look at the riot of colors around me.

"Yellow. Like the sun."

Mom grins wider.

"You got it, baby. When we're done here, we'll head to the hardware store for the yellow."

I smile and it's been so long, it feels like my face is cracking open.

It's almost closing time when we get to the hardware store to pick out my paint. Actually, it's *after* closing time, but Mom bangs on the glass door until the teenage clerk spots us. He takes one look at her in her paint-splattered cutoffs and his face gets red and he hurries to let us in.

I walk up and down the rows of paint swatches. Who knew there were so many versions of yellow! I start to worry that I'm taking too long, but the clerk, still blushing, tells us to take our time. Finally I see it, a bright yellow that is somewhere between the color of baby chick and lemon pie. I hold it out to Mom, and she gives me a very nerdy thumbs-up. I check the name, in case Gina asks, and when I read it, I know more than ever that this is it. My yellow is called Sunny-Side Up.

We paint until well past midnight under the glow of the overhead light and the pink tasseled lamp we moved in from the living room. After Mom goes to bed, I lift up Teresa and we have a talk. I tell her she is special and she is safe and that now is her time to be brave. Then I carry her out to the backyard and introduce her to her sisters. I dig her a new home right in the middle of the black-eyed Susans. Maybe she needs to be with her friends to help her grow.

Poetry and Music

THE SKY BREAKS OPEN, SPITTING BIG FAT DROPS of rain, and I wake to the sound of thunder. It rumbles so loud it shakes the light fixtures and rattles my chest. But my room greets me, even lovelier and yellower than when I went to sleep. I take a deep breath, catching the scent of lavender, and climb out of bed.

I stand in front of the mirror in the bathroom for a long time. I look the same. My hair is still short, maybe a little wilder now that it is long enough to see the beginnings of cowlicks, but it's basically the same. Same brown eyes. Same wide mouth I inherited from Mom. Same SpongeBob T-shirt I fell asleep in last night. But I feel different. Not fixed. That's not how this works. But I'm ready to try again.

I open the drawer where we keep the toothpaste and floss and old tubes of ChapStick and fish out the orange bottle. Then I let the water in the sink run cold and fill a juice glass. Before I can think about it too long, I swallow the little yellow pill that now matches my yellow room. I know it's not magic. Gina said so. But maybe it'll give me a fighting chance. If our dusty desert of a yard can grow a jungle of wildflowers, then I'm willing to believe anything is possible.

Mom and I spend the morning camped out on the red couch, eating crepes dipped in Nutella and watching reruns of *Parks and Rec*. The rain patters on the windows, and it makes me happy for my flowers. I say a little prayer for Teresa to drink her fill.

Near twelve, we hear a knock on the door followed by a crash and an *"Oof!"* A burglar wouldn't knock at noon on a Monday, but we creep around the corner from the living room anyway because we never lock our door. A very wet Sam is lying flat on his back in the hallway. He looks unharmed, but his cheeks are splotchy red like he's embarrassed. He couldn't look less like Nick in that moment, and for the first time, I feel myself relax around him. Mom and I each take a hand to help him up.

"So sorry. The steps were wet. I tried to call," he says as we lead him to the kitchen, away from the Nutella debris in the living room.

Mom thinks I don't know that she has been ignoring her phone for the last four days. But I see it on the kitchen counter, flashing the library's number over and over. I know it's the Tandy, demanding to know where she's been. She missed two days of work and was supposed to pick up a shift this afternoon for Sharika, who has gone to visit family over the long holiday weekend.

Sam takes a seat across from us at the kitchen table, making it look tiny. He has on what can only be described as a poncho. It's neon orange, like something you'd see on a grandma at Dollywood. Nick would never wear something so "uncool," but I kind of like it. And when he pulls it off to get to his laptop case underneath, I understand why he chose it. He has to keep his gadgets safe. He sets out the laptop and then an iPad. He spins the iPad toward me and clears his throat.

"I wanted to stop by and show you that app I was talking about, June, the one that helps the flowers grow," he explains. "We never got a chance to finish our conversation on Thursday, because of—" He stops, not knowing how to finish. I wonder when and what Mom has told him. I wonder if he stopped by before, when I was sleeping. I search inside for that old flame of fear and anger, but I can't seem to find it.

I touch the screen on the iPad. "Show me," I say.

We spend the next ten minutes scrolling through the various settings. It's basically Spotify for plants, and you can set it for daytime or nighttime and it plays music centered around what you think your plants might enjoy: jazz, classical, or nature sounds like babbling brooks and croaking frogs and birds of the jungle. I like the babbling brooks.

Sam spends the entire time talking only to me. Mom hardly says a word. When a little alarm clock on the iPad beeps, Sam shakes his head.

"I'm sorry, June, but I'm due at the library in fifteen minutes."

He packs up his bag and starts wrestling himself back into his orange poncho.

"Mom, aren't you supposed to work this afternoon?"

She looks away, toward the kitchen window and her phone, I notice.

"It's all right. I'd like to spend the rest of the day with you, Junebug."

"Mom, you have done nothing but spend time with me. I love you, but everyone's probably wasting away without your presence. Especially the teenagers."

Sam snorts from under his poncho.

"Work will always be there, June."

Mom can be stubborn. But so can I.

"The Tandy awaits," I say.

When Mom still doesn't say anything, I add, "Sharika's counting on you, right?"

She sighs. "I don't even know if Thelma is up for a trip in this weather," she says.

"I've got my Prius out front. I can drive you," Sam offers.

Of course he drives a Prius. But I don't find myself minding Sam so much now. In fact, I would *love* it if he would take Mom to work. She has been a little . . . clingy.

The two of us stare her down until Mom throws her hands up. "Fine. Give me two minutes. But June, you have to promise me you will lock the doors and call me if you need anything. *Anything*, okay?"

"*Okay*. Now go change!"

She darts down the newly coral hall to change and is back in less than a minute, pulling on a navy rain jacket over a yellow dress and looking exactly like the girl on the front of the salt container. Except the girl on the salt container doesn't have a buzz. I haven't asked her why she hasn't worn her wig. I guess she's waiting for me.

Sam leaves his iPad with me and promises to load the app on Mom's phone when he brings her back after work. After they leave, I pull on my rain boots and grab an umbrella and spend the next hour playing Miles Davis and frog sounds to my garden.

I'm back on the couch eating Nutella straight from the jar when the door creaks open again, an hour before Mom is supposed to get home. I sit up on my heels to peek through the window. But there's no one there. I creep down the hall and open the front door. A Ziploc bag with a light blue envelope inside rests against the screen. The plastic package glistens with raindrops.

I know this color blue. It's the same blue as Homer's dinner invitation. I shake the rain off and carry it to my room. Just holding it makes me feel itchy, because I don't know what's in it and I'm afraid it's a goodbye letter and I'm also kind of hoping it is a goodbye letter because that means I won't have to see Homer again and explain what happened at the parade.

I put two fingers to my wrist and check my pulse. Yes. Definitely fast. I sit with the feeling for a minute. I *think* this is a normal reaction that a person would have. Anyone would be jittery over a mystery letter.

I take a big whiff of Luis's calming lavender and open the letter.

It's a poem. Of course. I pause. The words are Homer's words, but I recognize the whatif parts from somewhere else. I shake my head. Why is it so familiar? Gina! Gina read a poem to me during one of our sessions. It's Shel Silverstein. And it's about this kid who can't stop worrying about all the things that might happen, like being dumb in school or not getting any taller or losing a kite or not making friends—all the whatifs. It is the story of my life.

Of all the poems Homer has recited at me, I never wanted him to choose this one. I never wanted to be the whatif girl, the worrywart (*such* a horrible name). I am already that girl to the kids at school, who have seen my scabs and know my hiding place in stall number three. I'm that girl to Gina. I'm even that girl to Mom, though I know she loves me no matter what. And now I'm that girl to my first friend. This is his goodbye for sure. I sniff a little and press a fist to my chest, right in the center, where it aches. And I keep reading.

He brings up the Tandy's rants and games of chess when I might win less (never going to happen). I surprise myself with a laugh. "Whatif" *is* the story of my life, but Homer's rewritten it. It's not a goodbye.

Will we really still be friends after what he saw on Thursday? And when school starts back? And soccer starts up? And there are no more endless library days? I read it five more times. But it's a whatif I can't answer.

15

Little Crowne Bakery

I'M STANDING IN FRONT OF THE COLUMBIA PUBLIC
Library with my blue hair tucked under my arm like a
football. I have not decided if I'm going to wear it again
or not. On the one hand, it's an electric-blue gift from
Sharika. On the other hand, it made Allyson call me
"Violet" from *Charlie and the Chocolate Factory.*

Mom leans against Thelma and waits for me to take
the first step forward. But I'm afraid. I'm not sure of
what, but it's there, that fear, as hard and uncrackable
as a walnut. Thelma's engine ticks. Mom's Juicy Fruit
snaps. I cannot move.

"I have an idea," Mom says, and pulls out her phone.
She squints at something, types some more, and then
slips the phone back into her pocket. "All right, that's
settled. Come on then."

I turn to her. "Come where?"

"You'll see."

It is 9:58. The library opens in two minutes.

"Aren't you going to get in trouble? Didn't the Tandy almost fire you yesterday?"

"No and no. I covered for Sharika and now Sharika is going to cover for me for a bit. Hop in." She tugs open Thelma's door and I crawl back in, grateful to have bought some time, no matter where we're going.

It turns out we're not going far. Actually, we could have walked. Just one street over and a quarter mile down, we pull up in front of a low row of shop fronts—an antique jeweler, an alterations shop, and right on the end, under a peachy scalloped awning, the Little Crowne Bakery.

White metal tables with curlicue designs sit out on the sidewalk next to an old-fashioned oven painted pale pink. Someone has turned it into a planter and filled it with bright purple petunias. A chalkboard outside the open door reads:

Today's Specials
Scone: Almond Raspberry
Tartlet: Lemon Meringue
Cake: Pink Velvet

Holy moly. Nix is *fancy*.

The bakery itself is tiny. There is just enough room next to the front window for one white round table and three chairs. A coffee station is set up underneath pink-and-white china plates hanging on the wall in the corner. The pastry counter is across from the open door. The pastry counter is *everything*.

I stand under the twirling fan and drink it in with my eyes. The glass case is filled with silver trays lined with red velvet cookies and carrot cake bars and double dark chocolate scones and butter cookies and flourless chocolate cake. There's a whole section with petit fours glazed in white and pink and yellow icing. No wonder Nix was so interested in Mom's free leftovers.

We order two almond raspberry scones from the girl behind the counter, who's playing a game on her phone and looks bored. We take a seat at the little table. She delivers our food on mismatched china plates that look like the ones on the wall and points us toward the napkins and utensils at the coffee station. The scones are delicious—crumbly and sweet with just the right amount of sour from the raspberries. But honestly, they're not amazing. They're not *unforgettable*.

"You could do better," I tell Mom between bites.

"Oh, could she now?"

I turn as slow as a person can turn and still be in motion. Nix stands behind me with her hands on her hips, wearing a frilly pink apron. The outfit's so shocking I forget to be embarrassed that I just insulted her in her own place of business.

"She didn't mean it," Mom says, fumbling with her napkin.

"Sure she did." Nix turns the last chair around and straddles it like a cowboy.

"Well," Mom says, and looks down at her plate. I have never seen her nervous in my whole life. I didn't even know she knew *how* to be nervous. And now she's tracing some complicated pattern through the crumbs on the table to avoid our stares.

Nix turns her eagle eyes on me. "Glad to see you out and about. Did Luis tell you I asked after you?"

"He did."

Has Luis seen her in this pink apron? With her hair twisted up and covered in a hairnet? I start to giggle. I can't help it. The laugh escapes like a bubble.

Nix narrows her eyes at me. "What's so funny?"

"Nothing," I say, swallowing. "You look good in pink."

Mom starts laughing now. It sounds a little hysterical, but at least she's looking up.

Nix winks. "Why do you think I play poker on my off hours? This much pink'll kill a person."

She turns back to Mom, who is still laughing and wiping at the corners of her eyes.

"Which leads me to you."

Mom freezes.

"I am tired. Tired of wearing pink and tired of getting up at the crack of dawn to get these doors open for the morning crowd. And I am tired of this menu. Did you know I have made some variation of the same coconut cake every week for thirty-four years?"

We shake our heads. We did not.

"I need some new blood, and not some *teenager* putzing around for the summer who doesn't know a snickerdoodle from a sugar cookie." She jerks her thumb toward the girl at the counter, who rolls her eyes without looking up from her phone.

"I need a pastry chef to create a menu that will not leave me sick and tired of life. And I need somebody to bake it all so I can play more poker."

"With Luis?" I ask.

"Yes, with *Luis*. You mind your own business, now." She turns back to Mom. "I tasted your petit fours. I talked to Sharika. I know what you can do."

"You talked to Sharika about my baking?" Mom sounds like someone has just stopped her on the street to ask for her autograph.

Nix nods.

Mom flaps her hands over the table. "But I don't have a degree. I never finished culinary school."

"Do I look like I give a fig about degrees?" Nix asks.

"No. No, you don't," I answer for Mom. "You should try her lavender ice cream and her croissant French toast and her crème brûlée."

"June!" Mom cries.

"What?"

"Oh, I aim to," Nix replies, and stands, effectively dismissing us. But when she walks us out, she slips Mom a card with her name and "Little Crowne Bakery" on it. It's pink.

Mom drives right by the library on our way back and has to make an illegal U-turn in the street. Thelma nearly takes out a telephone pole. I think Mom's in shock.

"Why are you so surprised that someone would want to hire you to be their baker?" I ask when Mom finally shuts off the engine in the library parking lot and leans her head against Thelma's steering wheel.

"I just never thought . . ." She trails off.

"Mom, you are amazing. Everyone says so. Have we ever had leftovers of anything you made in our entire lives?"

"But . . . I'm not legitimate," she says to the dashboard.

"What does that even mean?" I ask.

She still doesn't move.

"Mom, if Nix, who owns her own bakery and has run it for over thirty years, says you are legitimate, then you are le-git-i-mate."

She groans. I put my hand on her shoulder.

"Even if Nix never said it, even if you never work at Little Crowne Bakery, you are still a bona fide amazing baker and *everybody* knows it."

She finally sits up. There is a wrinkly line across her forehead from Thelma's stitching.

"You're better at the pep talks than me," she says, and opens her door.

"I am," I say, following her out, "and I think you should take that job."

I was so busy making sure Mom did not internally combust over Nix's offer, I forgot to be nervous about going back into the library. But the minute we step through the sliding-glass doors and into the lobby, I feel a shiver, and it has nothing to do with the air-conditioning. This is my first time back after the "episode," and I don't know how to *be* now that everybody knows.

I sprint up the stairs to the teen section, my home base. Sharika is sorting through books on Mom's desk. She must have gotten the assistant children's librarian, Marlene, to do story time so she could fill in for us during our unplanned breakfast. Poor kids. Marlene reads like Siri.

When Sharika sees me and Mom, she speed-walks over. Sharika refuses to run. She says it is undignified. If the building were on fire, Sharika would still be sashaying out like the queen of England. But when she gets to me, she wraps me in a most undignified hug and I manage it okay. After a minute, Mom has to tell her to let loose.

"Oh, honey. I am so glad to have you back," she cries, and then she *literally* cries and we have to walk her back around the desk where she will make less of a scene.

"Don't you do that to me again," she says, pointing a blue fingernail covered in tiny white stars at me, left-over glamour from the Fourth of July.

"I promise," I say, but honestly, that's the thing about all this. It's hard to promise something that's out of your control. "I promise to try," I add.

Mom touches her head to mine like we are trading secret thoughts.

I pull back and say, "Nix just offered Mom a job."

"Say what?"

When Sharika whips her head around to Mom, I make my exit. Running back down the stairs, I spot the Tandy and take a sharp left toward the sliding doors. She has just enough time to shout, "No running!" as I sprint through the lobby and back into the sunshine.

She probably thinks I am running away from her, the old bird. But I am not. I am running *to* something. I am running down the hill to my garden by the river.

16
Sticks and Stones

I KNEW HE WOULD BE HERE. HOMER. I STOP HALF-
way down the hill and watch him. My heart taps out
a crazy beat. What if he's already regretting his offer
to be my friend past this summer? And even if he's
not, it's not fair to do that to a person, sign him up
as one of my "safe people," when he doesn't have all
the facts.

He's kneeling in the dirt, cultivator in hand, running the forked ends in between the rows to rake neat
straight lines. He stops every now and then to pull
up a weed or dig out a rock, which he pitches into the
river. He's in the zone and doesn't notice me until my
shadow falls across his back. He is wearing the same
faded red T-shirt he wore on the first day I met him.

He sits back on his heels.

"Hi," he says.

"Hi."

I wipe my clammy hands on my shorts and take a step back.

He stands and brushes the dirt from his knees. When he tucks a curl behind his ear, I wish I'd worn my wig.

"I got your letter."

"Mine and Shel's," he says, and grins.

"Yours and Shel's."

I walk a ways away from the garden, hoping he'll follow. After spending yesterday afternoon playing music to my wildflowers, I feel like my plants have ears.

I head down to the river and slip off my flip-flops and dig my toes into the muddy water. The coolness helps me think. I pick up a rock and try to skip it, but it sinks with a plop. Homer takes his time searching for one. His skips five times.

I clear my throat.

"So, I need to explain this thing going on with me."

"You don't have to if you don't want to," he says, and man, do I want to take the out and skip rocks for the rest of the afternoon. But if we're going to be friends, real friends, he has to know.

"No, I . . . I think I want to." Why is this so hard? If I could write like Homer, then I'd just put it all on paper and hand it over and not have to say a word.

"It's kind of a big deal," I say, looking for a place to start. "It's bigger than poetry."

"Nothing's bigger than poetry," he says, and smiles.

I drop my rock. This was a huge mistake. How's a kid like Homer ever supposed to understand what it's like to be me?

"You don't get it. You can't, because you're a soccer star at a rich school with a nice house and a perfect family. But trust me," I add, "there are bigger things than poetry."

He freezes in mid-throw.

I want to gather all those words back and run away up the hill with them.

"You think I'm *rich*?"

"Uh, yeah," because uh, *yeah*.

"My mom teaches at a *community* college. And my dad teaches history at Oakwood and coaches the soccer team. He's the only reason they can afford to send me there. Faculty kids get half-price tuition."

"But you get an allowance."

"Which I work for."

"And you live in that nice house with the little fence and the porches."

"That was my grandparents' house."

"But—"

"How did you even know I played soccer?" he asks now.

My cheeks get hot, fast. "I heard some girls talking about it in the bathroom."

He shakes his head. "Why didn't you ask me about it?"

"Why didn't you *tell* me about it?" I shoot back.

"You didn't tell me your whole life story either."

He thinks his secret soccer status is the same as my secret whatif-girl status? His makes him cool and mine makes me friendless. A spark of anger sneaks into my voice.

"Homer, this is *not* the same. My anxiety isn't like, 'Oh, I hope I studied hard enough for that test.' It's getting four hours of sleep on a *good* night and thinking of every single bad thing that could happen on the walk from my house to the bus stop. It's . . ." I cringe. "It's hiding in the bathroom so I don't have to figure out where to sit during lunch. Do you know why I shaved my head?" I don't wait for an answer. If I do, I'll never get this out. "Because I used to pull my hair out."

It feels like the world's biggest secret. I wait to get hit with the screen-door smack of his reaction. But his face is unreadable. There's not even a flinch. So I keep going, like a dare, to see how much he can take.

"Full bloody hunks of it, Homer. It would come away in my hands and it would feel good because even though it hurt, it still hurt less than the thoughts in my head. But—" I shrug. "People started to notice the outside hurt and I knew I had to find a better way to deal with all of it." I throw my hands up, like *all of it* was this, us, but also the entire world and all the invisible worries in my brain.

I let my arms fall. It all feels too heavy all of a sudden, and I don't have the energy to explain. "On the morning of the very first day we met, I shaved my head because I wanted this summer to be the summer that changed everything. I was going to beat the anxiety and make it so Mom and I would never need anyone to make us happy but us."

Saying it now sounds impossible, two wishes too big for one body.

"I'm not a lion or a rebel or a superhero." I sit down right in the mud. "I'm just me."

Homer opens his mouth, but I hold up my hand.

"I think I'm getting better, but I don't know if I will ever be 'well,' if you know what I mean."

Homer stands exactly how he was. I wait for him to walk away. I want him to and I *don't* want him to at the same time.

He rolls the rock he's been holding between his palms, looking at it instead of me.

Finally he says, "I'm not very good at . . . at talking to people off the field. Nobody really . . . they don't care about the things I care about. It's why I never told a single person that I like poetry . . . until you."

I look up at him.

"I mean, do you know anyone else who would voluntarily spend the summer at the *library*?"

I raise my hand like I'm in math class. "Um, me."

His smile is almost invisible, but it's there.

"'You find sometimes that a Thing which seemed very Thingish inside you is quite different when it gets out into the open and has other people looking at it.'"

"Is that a poem?" I ask.

"No. It's Winnie-the-Pooh."

"You're quoting Pooh at me?"

He laughs and something in me settles back into place.

"I'm just trying to say thanks for sharing your 'Thingish' secrets with me."

"Uh, you're welcome?"

My cheeks feel hotter than ever. But this time it's only half out of embarrassment. The other half is happiness. He knows the worst of it and he didn't walk away. I take my time getting up.

I pick up a rock and toss it back and forth like him. "You know," I say, "with quotes like that, I might be doing you a favor, being your friend." I'm teasing. I wait to see if he knows I'm the kind of friend who can do that.

He smiles. He knows.

"'Sticks and stones can break my bones, but words can never hurt me,'" he chants.

"That is the biggest lie a poem ever told," I say, and sink my rock, again. I am a terrible skipper.

He nods.

"Let's throw stones, then."

17
The Tandy

GRUBS ARE FASCINATING. AND WORMS. AND ROLY-
polys. I never knew how much life was underground
until I starting digging around in the dirt. It's approxi-
mately one thousand degrees, but I am out here in my
library garden, just like I have been for the last two
weeks.

Something changed after the Fourth of July. Well, a
lot of things changed. One of them is that I can't stand
being indoors. My body wants to be out here. It's quiet,
but not silent. There are crickets chirping in the grass,
and birds tweeting back and forth in the trees, and dogs
barking in yards, and cars vrooming by in the distance.
It's noise, but it is *peaceful* noise.

Mom and I eat in the backyard now. We moved our
kitchen table out there right in the middle of the wildflowers. It's like a tea party in Alice's Wonderland every
day. And at night, I sleep with my windows wide open

and Sam's babbling-brook sounds playing on Mom's iPhone.

My favorite out-of-the-way place is this garden. Luis helped me plant tomatoes. I now know how to fertilize the soil and tie the tomato plants to their stakes with twine so they don't fall over. Nix talked him into squash and raspberries too. It didn't take much convincing. Luis is such a pushover when it comes to his "Nicole."

I keep my watering can hung from a tree branch so I can fetch water from the river whenever our garden is looking dry. The more I get my hands in the dirt, the less I have to fight the worry, like the act of turning over the soil is turning something over in me. When I told Gina that, she got teary but pretended to pick Rochester hairs off her pants so I wouldn't notice.

I pinch a pale grub between my fingers and we study each other—one dirt lover to another. I dub him Larry. He wiggles and then goes limp. I think he's playing dead. I carry him over to the riverbank, where the mud is soft and the shadows from the maple leaves dance across the water. When I set him down, he rolls himself in the mud. So long, Larry. I'll be seeing you.

I scramble back up the bank and dip my hands in the watering can and rub them on my head. There are times when not a lot of hair is a bonus. I sit against my favorite tree, the one with the trunk that curves inward to form the perfect backrest. I lean back and survey my handiwork. The black-eyed Susans are growing tall and proud. Dragonflies flit back and forth from the water to their deep yellow petals.

"What do you think you're doing?"

My pulse kicks up a notch. I dig my hands into the grass to keep them steady. *The Tandy.*

"I'm resting," I say quietly.

"I mean *that.*" The Tandy points a long, bony finger at the garden. It is the finger of death.

"I, uh, thought I—"

"I, I, I. This library isn't about *you*, June Delancey." She grimaces and squints at the garden. "Are those the flowers I told you to throw out?"

I don't answer. I couldn't if I tried. All the spit in my mouth has dried up.

She walks closer to the yellow petals waving in the sun. I scramble to my feet.

"This is not your private playground, young lady." She steps even closer. "This is the property of the Columbia Public Library."

The toe of her pointed black shoe is on my soil.

"This," she says, and leans over without breaking her gaze from me, "is unacceptable." I watch, paralyzed, as she yanks one perfect green-and-gold Susan out of the ground and shakes her.

"No!" I yell. The sight of my plant, roots dangling and leaves torn, sets something in motion. Something bad.

Everything is ruined. All my plans. All the plants I spent hours caring for. I tried to save them and it didn't work. It's the *one* good thing I tried to do, and I failed. I can't stop shaking. I can't breathe, either. The Tandy eyes me suspiciously, like she's not sure whether I am about to faint or throw up. I'm not sure either. It's the parade all over again. I have to get out of here. I have to get away.

My legs are wobbly, but I start to run. My vision fades in and out. I follow the tree line. I'm almost to the road when I stop. I have *never* stopped in the middle of a worry spiral before. I've never *not* let it take me. I bend down and put my hands on my knees.

Maybe it's Homer. Maybe it's the little yellow pill. Or my yellow room. Or my garden. Or Sam's music. Or Mom. Or Luis. Or Nix. Or Sharika. Or all of the above. I don't know. But something feels different. I always thought I was fighting myself and my own broken brain. But for once the anxiety feels separate from me. I veer away from the road and run toward the library as fast as I can.

The sliding-glass doors are too slow. I turn sideways and shimmy through. I don't know if Mom is upstairs or in the children's section or stocking books. I pause in the lobby, wanting to run in all directions. I dart to the front desk. I need something that will get to her faster than my feet. I pick up the library phone and press intercom. The speakers crackle.

"Attention! Attention! I need Corinne and Sharika . . .

and Homer, if you're here. Please report to the front desk. Stat!"

I don't know what "stat" means, but I have heard it on enough doctor dramas to know it makes everyone come running.

Mom is first, followed by Homer. She flies down the stairs, her skirts fluttering behind her.

"*What?* What is it?" She grabs my face. "June, are you okay?" I start crying. I can't help it. A body can only do so many brave things at a time.

Sharika comes running across the lobby before I can answer, her arms jerking up and down like a robot on high speed. Sharika is *running*. She stops next to Homer and puts her hands on her waist to catch her breath.

"It's the Tandy! We have to get down to the garden!" I shout. Mom and Sharika look confused, but Homer heads for the exit at a sprint.

We follow, bumping into Luis and Nix as they rush out of Conference Room C.

"What's the ruckus?" Nix says, looking from Mom to me.

"Luis, the garden," I rasp, out of breath.

Luis looks to the doors.

"It's Mrs. Tandy," Sharika adds.

That's all it takes to get everybody moving again.

We take the hill at a run.

Below us, Homer faces the Tandy in the garden. He's

crouched like a linebacker. She moves left and he moves right to block her.

"Betty!" Mom shouts from halfway up the hill, and it's just enough of a distraction. When she turns, Homer lunges for the sagging black-eyed Susan in her hand. She's so startled, she lets go.

"Corinne, this is none of your concern."

"If it involves my child, it *is* my concern," Mom says calmly enough, but she looks like she could breathe fire.

"I will not have people planting gardens willy-nilly on my property!"

The Tandy huffs and blows a frizzled hair out of her eyes. It's satisfying to see her sweat.

"*Your* property?" Sharika asks.

"The *public's* property," the Tandy corrects.

Nix joins in, drawing herself up to her full height so she looks like the queen of the forest. "If it's public property, why can't she use this space? What harm can a couple of tomato plants and some flowers do?" She does not mention the raspberries or the squash, thank goodness.

"Excuse me," Luis says, wringing a blue polka-dot handkerchief in his hands. "But you allowed me to plant my zinnias, yes? My zinnias have brought so much beauty to the bus stop."

The Tandy steps toward us, but for once, no one takes a step back. "That was different."

"Different how?" Mom asks.

While they bicker back and forth, I sneak around them into the garden. Homer lays the black-eyed Susan in my hands. She rests there like a lame bird.

"It will be okay," I whisper into her leaves, and walk along the edge of the garden until I find the pile of upturned earth where she had been uprooted. I place her carefully back into her home. While I scoop the dirt back in, Homer fetches the watering can from the tree branch and fills it with river water. We are trying to undo the trauma.

I don't hear how the conversation ends. But eventually, the Tandy marches back up the hill. When she does, Mom and everyone else move to Homer and me. She only got the one plant, for now.

"Mrs. Tandy says the board has to grant approval if we want to keep the garden," Mom says after a few minutes of silence.

I stare down at my Susan, her petals already a little dark around the tips and her leaves withered. We'll have to wait to see if she recovers. I can't let this happen to the rest of them. I cannot.

18

How to Play Chess

IT TURNS OUT THAT THE LIBRARY'S BOARD OF trustees meets on the first of every month. Which is how, on August 1, I find myself standing before Conference Room C in my best black dress with the white collar and swallowing a lump of fear the size of a grapefruit. They want to hear from me, "the girl who started the garden." I want to stow away in the recent returns shelf.

Mom, Sharika, Luis, Nix, Homer and all his family, and even Sam are here. Everyone is washed and clean in their Sunday best. I wish we could fast-forward to the end, *after* the meeting, so I can know how it ends. "Trustees" sounds welcoming enough. But what if I'm wrong? What if it's a roomful of Tandys instead? It's the whatifs that've got me worried.

"Take this. For luck." Luis hands me his polka-dotted handkerchief, and I tie it around my wrist.

"Don't let them intimidate you. Remember, four

afternoons a week, this room is a casino," Nix says, winking at me.

Mom and Sharika say nothing. They both look at me like they might faint.

The door creaks open and a small woman with hair almost as short as mine sticks her head out. "You're up next," she says, and disappears again.

I can hear them calling roll inside. There is a microphone. I am going to have to use a microphone. My palms are slick with sweat. They are on the *S*'s. Any second now.

I step away. I was wrong. I can't do this. I cannot. I am not a speechmaker. I'm the person who hides in the third stall of the bathroom and counts the bricks in the wall. I can't stand in front of a *roomful* of people *by myself* and talk them into keeping the garden. I can't convince anyone of anything. I have to make somebody else do it.

Homer stands next to me and opens his mouth to say something, but the door is opening and the woman is there again and she is motioning to me and saying something I can't hear over the rush of my own blood in my ears.

Homer steps between me and the door. I can't see the tiny woman. He bends down so our noses are almost touching. His tie is blue with little sunflowers all over it. A poetic choice.

"Listen, June. No one can save this garden but you."

"But—"

"No 'buts.' No one can save it but you, because no one cares about it as much as you."

"But—"

"Just think of it like a game of chess."

"What?"

I shift from foot to foot, trying to see around him. He moves like he did with the Tandy in the garden, blocking my view.

"You're the one who told me you always have to think five steps ahead, right?"

"Right," I say. Why is Homer Juarez, possibly the worst chess player in the world, giving me chess advice at a time like this?

"Just think about all the reasons the Tandy wants to tear up our garden and then tell the people in there why each and every one of those reasons is wrong. Knock them down like pawns." He makes a swiping motion with his arm like he's clearing the board, and his hand brushes mine. It starts my fingertips tingling. It's distracting in a whole different way. "That garden is *necessary*, June. All you have to do is prove it." He's right, and he's staring at me with such confidence that I will do and say the correct thing that I want to grab his hand, the one that touched mine, and drag him in there with me. Two is better than one.

But the woman is motioning at me again, just me, and he steps aside. I make myself walk toward her. I enter the room that should be so familiar but is strange at dusk with the sky fading to purple outside the over-sized windows. The adrenaline kicks in and I hope it's courage, not panic. Whatever it is, it moves my legs toward the front, toward that microphone.

As the big, heavy doors close, I try to reach back with my mind and feel all my people waiting outside in the hall. I step up to the microphone, too close, and bump into it. It screeches. I squeak and close my eyes. This is too much. I am not enough.

"Young lady?" I hear from the front. "Are you all right?"

With my eyes still closed, I picture myself standing on a chessboard. I am the queen. I am strong. I am fierce. I am independent. No one can make a move without me. This is my game to play.

I open my eyes.

At a long table across from me, the nine members of the Columbia Public Library's board of trustees sit and watch me. No one speaks. But a few smile. They are waiting for me to begin. I clutch the ends of Luis's handkerchief in my palm. I lock my knees so I won't fall over and then remember that's exactly what you're *not* supposed to do and bend them a little, like a runner on the starting line. It's time to win them over.

"Hello." The microphone is too high. I tilt my head up but it barely catches my voice.

A man, the one on the end in the navy blazer, removes his round glasses and blinks at me. "Don't worry about that thing. We can hear you all right," he says.

"Go on, dear," the tiny woman says.

I clear my throat and swallow and then have to make myself stop swallowing so I can talk. I step closer to the table. If I don't start now, I never will.

Move #1: remind them who they're up against.

"Umm, hello. My name is June Delancey and my mom is Corinne Delancey. She's the young adult librarian in this library."

I stop to cough.

"We know your mother. She's a fine librarian," the man in navy says. I take it as a good sign and my first successful move across the board.

Move #2: try to guess their argument and knock it down.

"Well, I'm here on behalf of my garden, the one down by the river. I know this is a public library on government land, meant to serve the people with its books and after-school and senior programs and all. . . ."

I start to trail off. What was I saying? What was the point? Why am I talking about old people? I shake my head to clear it. The man in navy raises his eyebrows.

Oh right, their argument. They're going to say this is a library, not a nature center.

"But, uh, I believe a garden can also serve people in the same way words can . . . by bringing them together to share a common experience. That's why I want this to be a communal garden, where anybody who comes to the library can come tend the land, too. The older folks can teach the little kids all about vegetables and the growing seasons. This could be one thing that everybody in all the different parts of the library can do together, no matter how old or young they are." The woman who led me in smiles big.

I pause to take a shaky breath and to bend my knees, which have locked up again. I thought it was supposed to get easier once you start talking. Isn't that what everybody says? I still want to throw up. I swallow the acidy taste in my mouth and get ready for Move #3: it's time to press my advantage.

"I know it requires maintenance, and the Tandy—"

The man in navy clears his throat.

"Sorry, *Mrs.* Tandy explained to me that your budget is limited. But . . . I promise to create a schedule so that it gets weeded and watered regularly and doesn't become an eyesore. It's a thing of beauty and I aim to keep it that way. I want any- and everyone to be able to stop by and sit awhile and enjoy shade and the company of the plants."

I try to get a feel for how I'm doing, but these people could beat Nix any day with their poker faces.

Move #4: find the weak spot.

"The truth is, these plants are *already* the library's plants. They started as a project in this very children's library and so, in a way, you could consider them your legacy."

A few people nod, so I keep going. I'm still terrified. But the only way to stop now is to get to the end.

"These flowers grew up here. They belong here. And I would be forever grateful if you would let them stay."

I smile, mostly with relief, because I'm done. I did everything I could and now I can leave. But a few more words bubble up before I can stop them.

"This garden basically saved me. I've, uh, had a rough summer. I made some plans and they didn't work out, and I get anxious when that happens." I wrap my arms around my own waist to stay steady. "It's not regular nerves like most people get. It's . . . more. But I'm working on it with the help of my mom and a lot of other people too."

My voice breaks on "too" and I take a second to clear my throat, but nobody hurries me. "Tending the garden helps me stop thinking about what might happen the next day or the next minute. It turns down the volume on my anxious thoughts so I can work around them." I force my hands to unclench and smooth down my dress.

"I just want to be able to keep taking care of the plants, because they take care of me, too. Please let the library garden stay. Please. If that would be all right by you."

It's a closed vote, so I leave them to it. I'm wobbly from that much talking with that many eyes on me. When I step back out into the hall, I take a deep breath like I'm coming up for air and kind of collapse into Homer.

He lifts me in a giant hug and I forget my name and purpose.

"How'd it go?" he asks when he sets me down.

"Well, don't go celebrating yet. But . . . here's hoping we won in four moves," I say, and grin. He takes my hand and squeezes, just like I hoped he would.

19

Goodbyes and Garden Parties

MOM HAS TO WORK THE VERY NEXT DAY, WHICH IS awkward given how we're in a battle of wills against the Tandy and everybody knows it. We manage to avoid her all the way until the end of the day. But when she gets on the speakers and announces that "the library is now closed" in her voice of doom, we know we have to do the BIG HARD THING we have been planning since the Tandy rampaged the garden.

On our way out, Mom stops by the front desk and says in as steady a voice as she can manage, "Betty, can I speak with you for a moment?" She's squeezing her purse so tight that her knuckles have turned white.

We practiced this over and over from the safety of our kitchen. But nothing can compare to the reality of the Tandy. This conversation is supposed to be polite and respectful and, as Gina put it when we called her this morning, "provide closure."

"What is it, Corinne? I'm quite busy," the Tandy says without looking up from her pile of late returns. Rumor has it that if you gather yourself enough late fees, the Tandy will revoke your library card. I don't know if that's true. But it feels true.

"Could we speak in the back?" Mom asks, her voice reaching an octave higher than normal. I wince. But she's doing the best she can under the circumstances.

"We cannot," the Tandy replies without so much as a pause.

The *one* time Mom *wants* to enter the dark recesses of the sorting room.

"Well, okay." Mom clears her throat. I move closer so she can feel my shoulder against hers.

"Let me guess. You need more time off," the Tandy says, drawing a big thick line under someone's name. "Or no, wait, you want me to rearrange everyone else's schedule, *again*, so you can have a *game* night with the *teens*." She says "teens" like you would say "gremlins."

"No, actually," Mom answers, letting out a long-held breath so the ruffles on her white scarf ripple. "I'm giving you my notice. I've taken another job, and it begins the first week in September."

The Tandy drops her pen. "You're moving to another library?"

"No, ma'am," Mom replies, standing up straighter. "I will be working in a bakery."

The Tandy purses her lips. "You're going to be a *waitress*?" she asks.

"She's going to be the head pastry chef!" I chime in.

The Tandy turns her eyes on me, her mouth flattening in that familiar line that means *Do Not Cross.*

"Is that so?"

Mom and I both nod.

The line sags and her mouth starts to quiver and I swear I have never seen anything like it in my life. The Tandy looks like she might cry.

"Please, Corinne. I'm sorry about the fuss over the garden. But your girl still got her day in court. Ha ha," she laughs. At least, I think it's a laugh. It sounds a little like she has a hair ball.

She places a hand on Mom's. I see Mom fighting not to pull away. "The truth is, you're the best young person's librarian I have ever had. We've never seen such participation in our theme nights and social events. And no more *vandalism.* Books are not only being checked out, they are being returned in *pristine* condition," the Tandy continues. Her voice is weakening, but it's hard to tell if it's genuine appreciation or tiredness at having to say nice things. "I used to have your spunk. I started in the youth section. Did you know that?"

Mom cannot hide the shock on her face. I don't even try.

Mrs. Tandy nods. "It's true. And I worked my way up until I became head librarian. I had big plans for this place. Book fairs and read-a-thons." She smiles with pride. "But then, budget cuts." Her smile slips. "And angry customers yelling at me because their holds didn't come in on time. And ridiculous book bans and roof leaks and heating repairs and"—she throws up her hands—"all the plans I had never happened. But you and your girl—you make things happen. Corinne, please, I ask you to reconsider."

Mom is a big softy and for a second, I think she'll crack and promise to serve the Tandy for the rest of her life. But she sticks to the plan, like we practiced, and gives a polite "No, thank you," and we beat it out of there.

It's a victory, for sure, because Mom is pursuing her dreams. But when I look back, I catch a look on the Tandy's face that I won't forget. She looks . . . lonely.

The following Monday, the board of trustees informed us that we would get our garden. I was so happy I danced backward down the nonfiction aisles. We won! We beat the Tandy and we will get to keep our garden *and* share it with the whole library!

But now, on this very last Saturday of August, the very last Saturday of summer before school starts again, I catch myself feeling sorry for the Tandy. *Mrs.* Tandy.

She's just trying to do right by her library, I guess. Even if she did try to annihilate my garden.

I'm sitting in the windowsill of the children's section, soaking up the mellow afternoon light and trying to picture her as a young person working in the library. Less lipstick on her teeth? Less clickety-clackety shoes and fingernails? More smiles? Maybe she got really crazy and actually *talked to people*. It's too bizarre to believe. I'm shaking my head when Mom comes down from the teen section for the very last time.

"You ready, Junebug?"

I hop down as Sharika shuts the overhead lights off, one by one. It feels like goodbye. But it's not like we're disappearing. Mom has already volunteered to do story time with the little kids on the days she has off from the bakery and game nights with the teens, and I've got my garden to tend and the recent returns to check on. Still, I stop and look around as Mom takes one of my arms and Sharika takes the other. This place is as much my home as our little white house with the cracked front steps.

We are almost out the door when something makes me stop. I turn back to the front desk, where Mrs. Tandy is shutting down the computers.

"Uh, Mrs. Tandy?"

I expect her to snap at me, say, *What do you* need, *Ms. Delancey?* When she just looks at me in silence, for a second I forget what I came to say.

"I just want you to know that if you ever need to blow off steam, or uh, whatever, you can come down and dig in the garden for a while."

She raises her eyebrows at me. "Thank you, Ms. Delancey. I'll keep that in mind."

She doesn't smile. But she doesn't *not* smile either.

I squeeze Mom's and Sharika's arms tight in mine and we nod at Mrs. Tandy, who waits a beat and then nods back. Then, together, we walk through the sliding doors and out into the fading light. But we don't go toward the parking lot, where Thelma waits in all her rusted glory. Instead we head for the hill and the line of trees and the river beyond. I have to help both of them make it down the slope, as they *insisted* on wearing heels for the occasion. Who wears heels to a picnic?

But as we approach the garden, I kind of wish I'd worn something other than my jean shorts. This isn't an ordinary picnic, after all. It's a *dedication party* for the garden that we all fought so hard to save. Earlier today we set up torches along the water's edge. And now that they're lit, they throw a golden glow into the blue night.

Nix is just laying out the red-and-white-checked blankets when we reach the bottom of the hill. It was Homer's idea to have the party on the last day of summer to celebrate our win.

"Ladies!" Luis cheers as we take out of his hands the lawn chairs that he was struggling to open. "You are all visions." He's right about Mom. She's in a rose-colored wraparound dress with a gold silk scarf around her neck. Her red hair is pinned in loose curls. We are both wearing our wigs tonight, even though our hair has finally grown out enough to be considered, well, hair. We like to save our wigs for special occasions.

Behind Luis, Nix rolls her eyes. "Stop flirting, old man," she says.

"My love, you know I only have eyes for you!" Luis exclaims, and we *all* roll our eyes, but I catch Nix blushing. Maybe it's real love after all.

I set out several baskets of food—plates of cold cuts and cheese, bowls of pesto pasta salad, beans baked with brown sugar, and a whole platter of fried green tomatoes with Mom's spicy aioli. I am especially proud of the tomatoes. They came right from this very garden. We just finished planting some pumpkin seeds too, to begin cultivating our crop for fall so the little kids will have something to pick come October.

I'm just straightening out the curried deviled eggs when something barrels into me like a cannon.

"Rochester, down!" Gina yells from farther up the hill. She's taking these tiny mincing steps like she has never been outside in her life. It's like watching a house cat in the wild. And even though Rochester is licking my nostril, I'm glad they came. I want all my safe people together tonight. Homer jogs up with his parents and sisters. As Lucy squeals at the sight of Rochester, I look at Homer and my heart thumps twice, extra fast.

He runs up to me. "Sorry we're late." He points a thumb at Kat. "*Someone* had to finish fighting with her boyfriend."

"Men," Kat sighs as I toss a piece of salami in the grass to distract Rochester.

"Tell me about it," Sharika sighs. Andy from the Jiffy Lube never did make an official date.

Behind us, Sam is easing his way down the hill with his trusty satchel at his side. He's waving like a goof. He's been coming around a lot lately, adding shows he thinks we'll like to our Netflix queue and helping me find new music for my plants. I can't believe he ever reminded me of Nick. Teresa is well and thriving now, and I have Sam in part to thank. I caught him once, sitting in the tall grass in the backyard, holding his iPad up in the air like a conductor and playing the Beatles at top volume. Mom still hasn't gone out with him. Even after I told her it was okay by me. She says she doesn't need a man to make her happy. She's *already* happy. And she wants it to be just us girls for now. That's okay by me too.

Once we are all assembled, we take advantage of the remaining light to get down to business, passing platters and bowls and spoons and pitchers of lemonade, before settling into a circle on the blankets with paper plates bowed with goodness. Luis and Nix sit behind us in the lawn chairs.

When there's not a slice of fried tomato left and everyone is sighing and leaning back to make room for their bellies, Mom lets me unwrap the dessert. It's her famous watermelon pie. Mr. Juarez pretends to make a grab for it, and Mrs. Juarez groans. But Mom smiles and sits up on her knees to serve. I'm in charge of passing it around.

Instead of sitting down when I'm done, I take my place in front of the bronze plaque that the people from the board made for me. It reads:

THE JUNE B. DELANCEY
CHILDREN'S COMMUNITY GARDEN
MAY ALL OUR HEARTS BE SO WELL-TENDED

I look around at my friends bathed in the rosy left-over glow of summer and torchlight and clear my throat. All eyes settle upon me. In this moment before I speak, with my heart thrumming and the river flowing steadily behind me, I make a final wish: *Let these people be my people forever*.

"I am not one for speaking my truths so publicly. Well, at least up until a couple of weeks ago."

Homer snorts into his pie and I do my best to ignore him.

"But I want to thank you all for coming out here tonight, on this last day of summer."

The words settle around us like dew on the grass.

"I am grateful to each of you for helping me save this garden from the Tandy." I shake my head. "Sorry, *Mrs.* Tandy."

Sharika and Mom bump shoulders.

"And I promise to keep tending it and I hope you'll keep visiting it too, along with anybody else from the library who needs some plant therapy."

I feel a flickering of nerves at what I'm about to say next, but it's the flash of a firefly, gone in a second.

"Thank you, also, for standing by me in times of crisis. And for seeing the real me."

I slip off my wig, let the cool of the night wash over me.

"I figured the best way to thank you was with my mom's food," I say, and Nix whistles. "So eat up and thank you all for being . . . you."

They cheer and raise their glasses to toast the plants and the food and the friendship and the summer that made it possible. I attempt a curtsy and then change it into a bow, which feels better.

When I settle back on the blanket, Homer leans over and whispers, "Couldn't have said it better myself."

I kick his foot with mine. Next week he will be back at Oakwood and I'll be starting middle school down the street. I have lots of thoughts on this. But before the whatifs can get me, I make myself practice what Gina said. I focus on the moment, sitting here on a blanket under the night sky with a belly full of food and surrounded by friends.

The crickets chirp and the fireflies blink and the flowers in the garden bend their stems in the gentle wind. For now, that's enough.

AUTHOR'S NOTE

This book is for the kids who worry. For the kids who think twelve steps ahead, for better and for worse. For the ones who have ever been told, like me, that they are "too sensitive." For the ones who feel those buzzy, itchy, nerve-racking thoughts even on the sunniest of days. Don't ever be ashamed of your anxiety. I'm not ashamed. Some of the best, most creative people I've known are anxious. Mental health must be treated with respect and care. We all deserve to be seen, to find our people, and to be free to be our honest selves.

ACKNOWLEDGMENTS

I could not have written this book without the support of my family. Jody, Charlie, Cora, Jonas—you all are the foundation, rock, shoreline (whatever metaphor you want to use) that keeps me grounded. Your steadiness gives me the freedom to dig around in the chaos of my imagination.

Reka Simonsen, you fit in with the steady group as well. We've done so much good work together and there is so much good work to come. You make me better. Always.

Keely Boeving, you understood June from page one. That alone kept me going.

Elysia Case, I have never cried over a cover until this one. You captured June's face in that moment of peace so perfectly that I wished I could step into the field of black-eyed Susans with her. Thank you. And Karyn Lee, thank you for your wonderful designs and for finding such talented artists for my covers so that every book shines its own light.

Afoma Umesi and Dolores Smyth, thank you for being early readers and champions of this story. You are both natural encouragers with sharp minds and excellent editorial glasses who aren't afraid to tell me what you really think. Thanks for the honest feedback.

To the folks at the real Triple Crown Bakery—thank you for letting me borrow your beautifully decorated locale (pink oven/planter included) and thank you for providing me with a steady stream of warm, magnificent cinnamon rolls. Sugar is a writer's best friend.

Last but not least, to my most favorite people—the librarians! This book would not exist without your presence in my life from the very beginning. My mom was my first librarian. At every book fair, she let me build a stack as high as her desk and even threw in some fruit-scented erasers to boot. I have met many great librarians since, more so now that I get to be on the other side of things as an author. Thank you for introducing the next generation to wonderful writers like Shel Silverstein and E. B. White and Beverly Cleary and to great characters like Winnie-the-Pooh and Miss Rumphius and the Boxcar Children and to all the new and diverse children's literature that I wish I had when I was a kid. These young readers are lucky to have you. Keep doing the good work. We love you.